CW01511746

Hither, Page

Page & Sommers, Volume 1

Cat Sebastian

Published by Cat Sebastian, 2019.

HITHER, PAGE

First edition. June 18, 2019.

Copyright © 2019 Cat Sebastian.

ISBN: 978-1099865343

Written by Cat Sebastian.

Chapter 1

The one thing everyone in Wychcomb St. Mary agreed on was that Mildred Hoggett was up to no good.

"I caught her snooping in the mailbag," whispered the postmistress, scooting to a seat nearer the other ladies in the doctor's waiting room.

"I heard she looked at Mrs. MacArthur's bankbook," confided the schoolteacher in tones of scandalous delight.

"Why couldn't she have found some other village to settle in?" lamented the president of the Women's Institute. "I do understand that it's been all but impossible to get good help since the war, but surely Miss Pickering could have found somebody else. There's no reason to bring *that* element into our midst."

Dr. James Sommers, overhearing this conversation as he left the examination room and prepared to call in his next patient, privately thought that if this Mrs. Hoggett were such a menace, the good people of Wychcomb St. Mary could very well hire somebody else to sweep their parlors and dust their bric-a-brac. But tradition mandated that the maid employed by ornery old Miss Pickering also serve as "daily woman" for several other households in the village. This was generally considered an eminently sensible arrangement, and even if it hadn't been, there were few people with the temerity to contravene Edith Pickering. Miss Pickering did exactly as she pleased, and if that entailed importing trouble-making charwomen from parts un-

1

known, then so be it. James himself had dutifully hired Mrs. Hoggett to clean the surgery three mornings a week.

James cleared his throat but the three women in his waiting room didn't seem to notice him.

"I do wish there was someone we could speak to. In an ordinary village, one might ask the vicar's wife to intervene," the postmistress said mournfully. She blew her nose, and James recognized the incipient signs of a winter cold sweeping through the village. Well, that would keep him busy, at least.

"Ha! Mrs. Griffiths barely manages to keep herself alive," said the schoolteacher, rapping her cane on the green linoleum floor for emphasis. "One never wants to ask her anything. The poor vicar."

"And those children. Perfectly feral, they are."

"If not Mary Griffiths, then who? Somebody has to do something."

All at once, the three ladies' heads swiveled to where James stood in the doorway. "Dr. Sommers," exclaimed the postmistress, clapping her hands together. "You're just the man—"

"Next patient!" he said quickly. He had not come to this village to serve as a mediator in internecine quarrels. He set broken limbs, prescribed ointments, and took temperatures. He kept regular hours, avoided any human interaction more complicated than afternoon tea, and read for exactly thirty minutes before bed. This was the closest thing to a rest cure he had been able to cobble together during the frantic sense of disbelief that had accompanied the end of the war—he was alive, England was still England, surely everything else would sort itself out in time. All that remained was to hang on to his fragile scraps of sanity—and by God, he was not letting them go in order to get knee deep in village squabbles.

However, when the next week he caught Mrs. Hoggett riffling through patient records when she ought to have been sweeping the waiting room, he realized with a sense of gathering doom that he could not let this go. That had made him very cross indeed, because all James wanted to do was keep his head down and avert his eyes from any unpleasantness, and here she was practically forcing him into action. With the gritted teeth of a man throwing himself into the breach, he asked the cleaning woman to come into the consulting room.

"Shut the door, if you please," he said.

"Oh my, I'm to be sent to Coventry, am I?" she asked, an expression of schoolgirl naughtiness out of place on her ordinary, middle-aged countenance.

"Nothing of the sort," he said. "I can't have you looking at patient records, so while I applaud your efforts to clean the room thoroughly, there's no need to clean within the file cabinet."

"I don't know what you're talking about," said Mrs. Hoggett. "You keep that cabinet locked."

Now James was thoroughly exasperated. He had deliberately chosen his words to avoid making the sort of direct accusation that would only mortify both of them. He assumed that she'd admit to overzealous cleaning efforts, promise not to open the cabinet again, and be grateful that he had spared her an embarrassment. This was not fair play on her part. "I do keep that cabinet locked," he said levelly. "I suppose the mechanism is faulty. I'll see to having it repaired." He resolved to keep the cabinet key safely in his pocket from then on.

He took a steadying breath and went on. "I know you come from London, but in a small village, it's important that people keep what little privacy they can manage. We're all in one another's business as it is," he said, feeling like an impostor in saying *we,* as if he belonged more than she did, when the truth was that he was almost as much a newcomer as Mrs. Hoggett. They had both come to Wychcomb St. Mary like animals scrabbling for shelter after a storm—she, after her London flat was bombed; he, after the war left him unfit for much else. "We need to keep one another at arm's length in whatever small ways we can manage. It keeps things peaceful, you understand." James knew well that everyone had secrets that ought to stay covered up. A stone in the prettiest, best-kept garden hid things one was better off not knowing—best for everyone not to lift that stone at all. "You understand?" he repeated. She made no response, but he hoped his words would serve as a warning.

They did not. Shortly thereafter he noticed that the contents of his medicine cupboard—not the one in the surgery, but the one upstairs in the washroom next to his bedroom, where Mrs. Hoggett had no business being—had been subtly rearranged. He fabricated a barely plausible excuse and informed the charwoman that he no longer required her services. She didn't deserve that polite fiction, but James was dedicated to preserving the illusion that there was nothing amiss in the village.

Yet he was uncomfortably aware of the fact that while Mrs. Hoggett might no longer be snooping in his own cabinets, she was almost definitely snooping in somebody else's. He briefly considered that he might have a duty to tell her other employers, but came to the conclusion that it was best to let sleeping dogs lie. Besides, that conversation he had overheard in the waiting room suggested that everyone was well aware of the cleaning woman's tendencies. Perhaps this wasn't a problem at all. Perhaps all the more troubling secrets would remain hidden from view. James did not think he had the mental wherewithal to cope with any mishap more dramatic than a chipped teacup.

So it was that when James learned that Mrs. Hoggett had been found dead at the bottom of the stairs at Wych Hall, he felt that his carefully constructed illusion of peace was in tatters. He dreamt, as usual, of the war. But this time the smell of mortars and blood infiltrated his quiet home, strips of flesh and lifeless bodies littered the streets of Wychcomb St. Mary. When he woke he wished he had not slept at all.

AFTER NEARLY A DECADE of living out of suitcases, Leo Page had it down to a science. He knew that his spare revolver fit neatly inside his shaving case, and that if he rolled his clothes up tightly, he could fit four shirts and a pair of trousers into a single valise with room for a book that he'd never get time to read. He'd carried the same copy of *Middlemarch* to Vienna, then Cairo, and back to England without getting past the first chapter. Maybe that would change now that he was in London, although it was hard to imagine a future that involved time to read anything other than a dossier.

When he received the telegram calling him back, he wondered if it was time to get a flat and whatever it was one put in a flat. Bedsheets. A kettle. Maybe a cat. He was vague on the details of how people lived during peacetime. It was December 1946, and he hadn't spent more than a month in the same place since the beginning of 1937.

He emerged from Victoria Station to find the city blanketed with a thick, filthy fog that obscured the gaps in the skyline where buildings had been hit by German bombs. Walking even the short distance to his destination in this weather was an unappetizing prospect, so he hailed a cab and in due course was deposited in an unremarkable street. The only thing distinguishing number 27 from the buildings that flanked it was a brass plaque by the door reading "Malvern Shipping and Surety." Leo tipped his hat to the porter and climbed into the decrepit old lift. On the sixth floor, he got out and began wending his way through semi-abandoned corridors until he reached the suite of rooms that was his destination.

A dark-skinned brunette a few years his junior looked up at his approach. She sat at a desk that held nothing but a black Bakelite phone, a pen, an inkwell, and a calendar. She regarded him blandly before forming her thin lips into something it took him a moment to interpret as a smile.

"He's waiting for you, Mr. Page."

This was a new agent playacting as secretary. He briefly wondered what had become of the last one—was she in the field? Dead? Compromised? He dismissed the thought. Thinking about the fate of people in his line of work was too dismal for a brisk autumn afternoon.

"Shut the door, Page." Sir Alexander Templeton barely glanced up from the stack of papers on his desk. He was a large man with a hairline that crept further back on his head each time Leo saw him. He looked like he ought to be dandling grandchildren on his knee and giving out butterscotch sweeties rather than organizing international espionage, but Leo knew Templeton worked hard to cultivate that appearance. "Well done in Cairo."

"Thank you, sir." He had foiled one assassination and instigated quite another one, then made the whole affair look like a lovers' spat, which anyone had to admit was a nice touch. He resisted the urge to buff his fingernails on his lapel.

"Take a seat."

Leo sat, his suitcase leaning against the leg of one tatty chair. Somebody had taken care to ensure that even the furniture looked ineffably like it belonged in the headquarters of a modest shipping firm. The battered desk, the mismatched chairs, the photographs—undoubtedly of strangers—in cheap tin frames, sooty windows still half covered by blackout curtains: nobody would guess that Templeton was a man of importance or power. Leo would have bet fifty quid that Templeton had amused himself greatly in outfitting this room.

Templeton finally looked up. "One of the fellows we've been keeping an eye on had a dead charwoman turn up at the bottom of his stairs. Dashed nuisance, police everywhere, had to scramble to make them think it was an accident. I don't like dead bodies turning up when we're trying to keep a low profile."

"No, sir."

"According to the medical examiner, she'd taken enough Veronal to fell a stallion and washed it down with neat gin. Then, for good measure, she took a header down a flight of stairs onto a marble floor."

Leo winced at the clumsiness of it all. "Not a professional job, then."

Templeton snorted. "Could be that an operative amused himself by making it look a bloody mess."

"Whose house?"

"Colonel Bertram Armstrong. One of the fellows we suspected of giving the Germans a helping hand in Dieppe. He's taken a fancy to playing the country gentleman at his ancestral pile, but he's still on the board of the steelworks his father owned. Confidential information about British steel production has turned up in some very unsavory places, and I'd damned well like to know how. Have it narrowed down to a couple of suspects, and I'll be honest that Armstrong seems the least likely—lazy old bastard. If it weren't for Dieppe, I'd ignore him. I'd like Armstrong to have enough rope to hang himself with, which is damned unlikely if he's got Scotland Yard crawling everywhere."

"I see," Leo said. Presumably one of Armstrong's men had planted false information with Armstrong and other suspects. It was a common strategy: several people suspected of leaking secrets were given information that differed only slightly, sometimes by as little as a single digit or differing typeface. Then intelligence services waited to see which version started to pop up where it didn't belong. It wasn't a tactic that worked well on professional spies, but it fooled amateurs—starry-eyed idealists without proper guidance, greedy profiteers, and other assorted fools.

Templeton let out a long-suffering sigh. "It might not even be Armstrong himself. Could be anyone with access to his papers. Could be the secretary, could be the housekeeper, and in a little village like that it could be damned near anybody, what with people in and out of one another's houses willy-nilly." The man squeezed the bridge of his nose. "Wretched places, villages. I have an agent posing as his maid, but if bodies are turning up hither and thither, we need to nip that in the bud. Draws too much attention."

Leo was brought up short. "You already have somebody there?" The situation as Templeton had described it hardly merited one agent, let alone two. Leo usually worked alone, and overseas. This was a far cry from the type of job he liked to think of as his specialty, and it was for this that he had been called back? "What exactly do you need me to do?" he asked slowly.

"Make sure there isn't some kind of serial killer or murderous cat burglar on the loose in the Cotswolds. Do whatever it takes to make Armstrong think he isn't going to have the police looking into his business." He paused and looked Leo directly in the eye. "It's a watching brief."

Templeton knew perfectly well that "do whatever it takes" and "watching brief" were pretty damned contradictory instructions. During the war they had all turned a blind eye, but the war was over. "A watching brief," Leo repeated.

"Settle down, Page. I'm not asking you to assassinate Englishmen on British soil." Templeton stroked his mustache. "Might be a nice change of pace for you after the past few years. Tiny village, right on the edge of the Cotswolds, probably very picturesque or something. Wychcomb St. Mary. Nearly a holiday for you. Don't you have people in Worcestershire?"

Leo furrowed his brow. "Sir?" They both knew he had no people whatsoever. No parents, no siblings, not so much as a stray maiden aunt. And then he realized what Templeton meant. "No," he lied, because that was what he did best.

"Or did that fellow die?" Templeton murmured, ignoring Leo's denial.

That fellow had been a colleague, briefly a lover, currently a skeleton in a graveyard in France. But that wasn't the point. The point was blackmail, and few people knew how that worked better than Leo Page. Maybe Templeton hadn't meant to black-mail him, but secrets were Leo's stock in trade. He ferreted them out, then used them to make people behave in the inter-ests of king and country. And if that required a bit of blackmail and death, a few lives ruined, a few others changed forever, so be it. Being able to care about that sort of thing was a nicety Leo hadn't ever had the privilege to observe.

"Wychcomb St. Mary, then," he said with a tight smile.

"Come, Page, don't act like that," Templeton said in a man-ner that he probably thought was disarming. "All I mean to say is that none of us exactly play by strict adherence to the law."

"Understood, sir," Leo managed, teeth clenched. He didn't give a fig for strict adherence to the law, or even lax adherence to the law, for that matter. What he cared about was that Tem-pleton clearly had an agenda of his own and wasn't sharing a tenth of it with Leo.

"Listen." Templeton held out a cigarette box to Leo, who took one. "This is how it is. Now that the war is over, they're talking about merging us with MI6. If that happens, then I'm out. I'm too old to play another man's tune."

Leo didn't like that one bit. He didn't have a knack for sen-timent, but Templeton had been the one constant in his life since the man had dug him out of a Bristol jail half a lifetime ago. Leo was conscious of harboring vaguely filial feelings for the older man, despite the fact that they likely hadn't strung together more than a dozen honest words between them in all those years and had rarely seen one another outside this building. He didn't care for the idea of the old man being cast out on his ear after damned near thirty years of doing the sort of work nobody in their right mind would sign up for. Still, Templeton had enjoyed free rein over this small, dirty corner of international espionage since the last war, and Leo ought to have foreseen that this arrangement couldn't last forever.

But there was something else gnawing on the edges of Leo's consciousness—or conscience, even, if his moth-eaten sense of duty could be called that—a vague uneasiness with the idea of acting on the intelligence of anyone he trusted less than Templeton. Leo was a weapon, and he didn't care for the idea of being aimed by a stranger.

Leo lit the cigarette and took a long drag from it. "So, our goal is to make MI6 forget we even exist," he said. "You want to fly under the radar until the bureaucracy moves onto solving some other problem. Which means that we either make the British steel industry look as if it's run by choir boys, or we present the entire case to them wrapped up right and tight, and hope they're too grateful to bother dismantling us."

"Precisely," Templeton said, and Leo felt something embarrassingly like devotion stir in the dustier reaches of his heart. "I knew you'd understand."

Chapter 2

Leo stepped off the train into a scene that would have made a decent picture postcard in almost any other weather. If there had been leaves on the trees or snow on the ground, Wychcomb St. Mary might have presented an inviting, if slightly predictable, prospect. But now the trees reached up from barren ground to wave naked, spindly branches in the leaden sky. The buildings he could see from the station platform were made of Cotswold stone that ought to have been a warm honey color, but had deteriorated to an ashy gray after years of exposure to soot and damp. The world was brown and gray, and even the people milling about the station platform were clad in faded shadowy hues.

Good, he thought. It was meet and proper, a fitting backdrop for the sort of work he had to do. Anything more cheerful would have made him feel like the grim reaper at a village fete.

But as he walked down the high street toward the inn, he was brought up short by the sound of a Christmas carol playing on the wireless inside one of the shops. Oh, hell. He knew it was December, but in the midst of his irritation with Templeton and his rush to outfit himself for this case, he hadn't quite taken stock of the fact that he'd be in England for Christmas. There were going to be mince pies and mulled wine; he was going to have to be jolly, heaven help him. Maybe he'd be lucky and have this case wrapped up before people really got into the thick of the season.

He scanned the street for any further evidence of yuletide cheer, as warily as he might search for enemy snipers. A paper chain hung inside the window of the stationer's, interlocked loops of red and gold. Leo suppressed a mad urge to walk into the shop and tear it down, announcing that Wychcomb didn't deserve festive paper. There had been a murder here, or at the very least a suspicious suicide. This was a place of death; no different from all the other places Leo had been sent over the past decade.

On the train, he had familiarized himself with the witness statements. The late Mildred Hoggett had been a charwoman who lived with a pair of spinsters on the outskirts of the village. The two old ladies, Miss Pickering and Miss Delacourt, didn't have enough work to keep the charwoman busy, so she spent her mornings cleaning other houses, including those of the doctor, the vicar, and the colonel. On the night of her death, she had been hired to work an extra few hours at the colonel's house, Wych Hall, to help his housekeeper and maid with a dinner party. Guests to this party included the two spinsters the victim lived with, their teenaged ward, the vicar, and the vicar's wife. The colonel's secretary, who lived at Wych Hall, also attended. The doctor had been present in the drawing room before the meal but was called away to a lying in, to which the colonel's housekeeper also went, as the new mother was her sister. Dinner proceeded without event. At the end of the meal, when the guests were leaving the table and progressing toward the drawing room, the victim's body was found at the base of the stairs, newly dead. All the guests claimed not to have seen anyone slip away alone, but all agreed that nearly any of them had the opportunity to go up the stairs under the guise of using the upstairs washroom, and that such an absence might have passed unnoticed. During the post mortem, it was discovered that the victim had recently consumed more than twice the usual dosage of a commonly prescribed barbiturate. She also had several contusions that were consistent with a fall down the stairs, but the coroner could not rule out a blow to the head from the proverbial blunt object.

None of the witnesses could suggest a possible motive, nor did any of them think Mrs. Hoggett had enemies. Leo had actually laughed out loud at that, drawing a sharp look from the other man in his train compartment. Walking along the high street, he wondered how many of the people he passed had loved ones who would cheerfully murder them given half a chance. He generally operated on the assumption that the only factor holding people back from widespread slaughter was fear—of the gallows, of damnation, of being thought not quite nice by one's neighbors.

Wychcomb St. Mary had a single inn, the Rising Sun. Leo gave his own name to the buxom woman who was stationed by the front door. It was, after all, only a watching brief—if one interpreted "watching" to include "watching someone down the barrel of a revolver"—and it was best to make occasional use of his own name so all traces of Leo Page didn't drop off the map entirely. Anyone who inquired into his background would discover a minor functionary in one of the less notable offices of the Ministry of Foreign Affairs with an unremarkable war record and an interest in bird watching that led him to take holidays in odd places. Leo felt a sort of affectionate embarrassment for this version of Leonard Page.

Alone in the room, Leo unpacked his valise, hiding his spare revolver on top of the wardrobe and neatly placing *Middlemarch* on the bedside table. Then he changed out of his town clothes and into a pair of secondhand corduroy trousers and a tweed coat he had bought yesterday in London after being briefed, tucked his favorite pistol into his arm holster, and went back outside to find a murderer.

MRS. HOGGETT HAD BEEN dead for over a week before they had the funeral. First, there had been the inquest, then some confusion regarding whether Scotland Yard or the local constabulary had jurisdiction. That scuffle had ended in neither body doing anything at all, which was just as well as far as James cared. He was acutely aware that the rest of the village was in a state of delighted curiosity regarding whether the woman's death had been an accident, suicide, or even—here the gossips' voices dropped to a thrilled whisper—*murdered*. This was by far the most excitement the village had seen since the sheep-stealing incident of 1935.

James supposed he ought to want to see justice served, that if indeed Mrs. Hoggett had been deliberately harmed, he ought to want her killer found and punished. But his moral compass seemed to be poorly calibrated—he could add that to his list of invisible war wounds—and he couldn't see any use in looking too closely into the matter. If Mrs. Hoggett had been killed, then perhaps it was because she had learned something dangerous in the course of her snooping. Surely, it was for the best that such a dangerous secret remain deeply buried, that way everyone could go back to their regular lives. He knew this was his mind grasping desperately at the status quo, but knowing this didn't make the urge any less intense.

The delay had the result that everyone was more or less over the initial shock by the time they gathered around the freshly dug grave, listening to the vicar say all the usual things. As James glanced at their faces, he thought they looked more bored than mournful. This was the tedious part of death, after all, standing about in the cold, water seeping into one's shoes from the damp earth. Perhaps they simply hadn't cared for Mrs. Hoggett enough to grieve her passing—she was hardly a beloved figure. Or maybe it was just that they had all become resigned to death over the course of the war; everyone had lost people in battles and air raids and sunken ships. Even Edith Pickering and Cora Delacourt, who had lived with Mrs. Hoggett, didn't seem terribly moved, but then again they had a good deal of practice in losing people, having lived through the last time the world decided to kill off a generation.

Next to Cora and Edith was Wendy, their ward, who seemed even more of a ragamuffin than usual in somber clothes and a hat that looked older than she was. Colonel Armstrong was there and beside him Edward Norris, his secretary. The vicar's wife was somewhere behind James, half-heartedly attempting to contain her children.

The wind whipped across the graveyard and James wrapped his muffler more tightly around his neck. He thought Mrs. Hoggett might have been gratified to see the great and good of Wychcomb St. Mary all freezing themselves like this. She would have liked the attention.

These uncharitable thoughts were interrupted when three things happened at once. Polly Griffiths, the vicar's daughter, wrenched free of her mother's grip and scampered helter-skelter across the graveyard. Colonel Armstrong, who for the past quarter hour had looked bored and distinguished, very much as if he were confident that his presence elevated the tone of the gathering, suddenly stood up straight and sucked in a breath of air that James could hear even over the hiss of the wind. And James caught sight of a stranger perched on a gravestone, sketch pad and pencil in hand, evidently drawing the church. The stranger's hat was pulled low over his forehead, but James had the creeping sense that he might have recognized the stranger if he were anywhere other than a country churchyard. This resemblance made it hard for James to remember that he was in Wychcomb St. Mary, not a blood-soaked field hospital. He could almost smell gunpowder and disinfectant instead of crisp cold air and smoke from the nearby vicarage chimneys.

This experience was far from uncommon. He knew this as a provable, scientific, medically sound fact. Every week he reassured patients that these lapses did not indicate unsoundness of mind. But at the moment his mind felt pitifully unreliable. He was clutching onto reality with his fingernails. He filled his lungs with clean, cold air and let it out slowly.

Wendy came up beside him and shoved a cold metal flask into his hands. The unexpectedness of the gesture jolted him back to the present. "You're fifteen years old," he hissed. "This'll make you go blind."

She raised a dark eyebrow. "Is that so, *doctor*? Besides, I'm not really drinking. I found it on Mrs. Hoggett's dressing table when I was clearing out her room. I thought I ought to take it away before Edith felt inspired to give the household a lecture on the wages of sin and the evils of strong drink."

He looked at the flask in his hands, and indeed he recognized it as the battered steel flask from which Mrs. Hoggett was wont to take covert sips when she thought nobody—especially her employer, Miss Pickering—was looking. "Surely you don't need to do that already. Clear out her room, I mean."

"Emptying it isn't any stranger than knowing it's just sitting there, and she'll never come back to it. Besides, I didn't go through with it. I took the flask and left almost everything else alone."

As she spoke, her brow furrowed. It occurred to James that during the year they had lived side-by-side at Little Briars, Wendy and Mrs. Hoggett had become if not friends then at least used to one another, despite the difference in their ages.

"Seemed I ought to bring it and properly pay my respects, as it were," Wendy was saying, sniffing the flask skeptically. "She always said it did her a world of good, but it tastes like what you gave me when I had worms."

"How much did you have?"

"Just a nip before we left the church. Come on, everyone's leaving. We don't have to stay any longer."

"Who's that fellow over there?" James asked. "The one sketching the church. I can't place him, but he looks familiar."

Wendy tipped back the brim of her hat and squinted at the man. "The fellow behind Mr. Marston? I've never seen him before."

"That's what I thought." But the more James thought about it, the more certain he was that he had indeed seen this stranger before. He took a step nearer to get a better look. Even beneath the bulk of his overcoat, the man was visibly thin. He had dark hair and tawny skin that suggested a recent holiday someplace sunny.

"Funny that Mr. Marston came," Wendy said. "I can't remember the last time I saw him out and about. I think he trimmed his beard for the occasion. Mrs. Hoggett would have been touched." She took another pull from the flask and winced, then gestured with her chin toward the man with the sketchpad. "Your stranger is getting kidnapped by Mary." Indeed, the vicar's wife was shepherding the man toward the house. "Looks like he's being carted off for tea and stale biscuits at the vicarage with the rest of us. So you'll get a chance to see if you know him after all."

LEO HAD HOPED THAT by loitering in the churchyard he'd get taken up by the vicar or his wife, and his plan had worked better than he expected. He gladly let himself be swept along from the churchyard into the vicarage along with the funeral-goers.

"Daniel," Mrs. Griffiths said, "This is Mr. Page." She brought Leo to a man of about fifty who wore rumpled clerical garb. His gray hair stood up in improbable angles on one side of his head, and it looked like he had shaved with neither a looking glass nor the slightest interest in the results. "He's writing a book on—what was it, Mr. Page? Owen, put down that cat or it's straight to bed for you!" She scurried off to rescue the cat from the arms of a small boy.

"Stone tracery in the Cotswold wool churches. More of a pamphlet, really." He held up his sketchpad. "Likely not very thrilling except to fellow students of church history," he said with a sheepish shrug. He had deliberately picked a topic too dull to inspire unwelcome questions and too obscure to have his ignorance challenged. Usually, he relied on bird watching as a cover story for why he was poking around, but for a bird watcher to come to Worcestershire in December strained credulity.

"You'll want to talk to Dr. Sommers, then," the vicar said, shaking his hand distractedly and jutting his chin in the direction of the man Leo thought he had recognized in the graveyard.

Leo most definitely wanted to talk to the doctor. Having been called away from the dinner party to attend a patient, Sommers was the only person connected with the dead woman with a halfway decent alibi. Also, if Sommers was who Leo thought he was, then he was responsible for a tidy little scar on Leo's right arm. Likely Sommers had sewed up many a bullet wound during the war and had long since forgotten the faces of his patients, but there was a chance that Sommers would remember the encounter as well as Leo did. If that were the case, he wanted to find out sooner rather than later.

"Sommers, there you are," the vicar said. "Mr. Page is writing about those bunnies of yours."

Leo turned in time to see Dr. Sommers blush a lovely shade of pink. He was every bit as handsome as Leo remembered: broad shoulders, wavy hair the color of caramel, warm brown eyes, and a mouth that gave Leo very distinct notions. He looked younger than he had when he spent that night in Caen fishing a bullet out of Leo's bicep, but everyone seemed younger when they weren't in the middle of a war. He supposed it was regular sleep and not being shot at that worked the magic, which meant he wasn't about to find out firsthand any time soon.

"Leo Page." He put out his hand. "Your bunnies?" he asked, arching an eyebrow. Sommers' hand was chilly from the outdoors. Leo let the handshake go a moment too long, watching the blush creep back into Sommers' cheeks. Well, well. Perhaps this case would not be entirely tedious.

"He means the three hares, our most notable church window, of course."

"Of course," Leo echoed, trying to sound like he knew this already. He really ought to have stuck with the bird watching excuse.

"My uncle was the vicar before Griffiths here. He made quite a study of that window."

That didn't explain why Griffiths called the window *your bunnies*, but Leo wasn't going to press the point. He'd happily let the conversation drift away from this window he ought to have known about. "You grew up here, then?"

That shouldn't have been a difficult question, but Sommers furrowed his brow. "I lived with my uncle during school holidays," he said. Then he tilted his head a bit and squinted his eyes as if trying to place Leo.

"I'm so sorry to hear about your Mrs. Hoggett," Leo said.

For some reason, Sommers fell silent. "It was kind of the Griffiths to do this," he finally said, with a faint air of defensiveness, as if Leo had wondered aloud why they were all standing about awkwardly. "Nobody wanted to send Edith and Cora—that's Miss Pickering and Miss Delacourt, over there on the sofa—home directly after the funeral. Mrs. Hoggett lived with them."

Leo murmured his assent and regarded the two older ladies. They had been mentioned in the dossier, so he knew who they were. The fluffy one in the fashionable hat was Miss Cora Delacourt, who had figured prominently in the scandal sheets of nearly half a century earlier. The other lady, an almost wraithlike presence with iron-gray hair and an ensemble evidently cobbled together from several decades' worth of mourning attire, had to be Miss Edith Pickering, a native of this village.

"Who's that large man standing behind them?" Leo knew from the dossier that it was Armstrong, but he wanted to get Sommers talking.

"That's Colonel Armstrong, and the fellow beside him is his secretary," Sommers said. "Edward Norris."

"That fellow is a secretary?" Leo couldn't help but stare at the young man. The photograph in the dossier hadn't done him justice. Blond hair, chiseled jaw, easily six feet tall. He looked like he belonged in the pictures—or rather he would if he didn't have the air of a man trying to fade into the wallpaper. It wasn't every day one saw a man so handsome look so damned rabbity. "Shouldn't he be in advertisements for shaving soap or hair tonic or something?"

Sommers' soft chuckle made Leo absurdly proud of himself. "The ladies are properly appreciative," Sommers murmured.

"Only the ladies?" Leo asked easily, casual enough that he could pretend he hadn't said anything indiscreet, but enough of a hint that a like-minded man wouldn't miss it.

Leo expected the doctor to blush, but instead, he bit his lip and gave Leo that inquisitive look again. Leo would have wagered that he was wondering if he had seen Leo in the sort of club that catered to men of their pursuits. Lord, what must it be like to have a face like that, to have all your thoughts and feelings written there for all the world to see? Such a liability.

"What about the bearded fellow?" Leo asked, indicating a man who had his arms crossed and his brow furrowed as he glowered in the corner. His hair looked like it had been cut with a kitchen knife and a beard obscured the lower half of his face. In a stage drama, he'd be the murderer, no question.

In fact, as Leo glanced around the room, he felt like he had indeed walked onto a stage set. The vicarage parlor looked like it had been furnished at a jumble sale some thirty years ago and was now in a state of shabbiness that was very nearly tattered, but it had the kind of comfort that invited muddy boots and dirty dogs and generally made one feel welcome. A meager fire sputtered ineffectually in the hearth, and the room would have been chilly if it hadn't been filled with people. They drank from mismatched, chipped cups that had likely seen hundreds of gallons of tea over the years. These people shouldn't have gotten mixed up in the sort of predicament that required the likes of Leo Page. It was all wrong. He hoped his next assignment would be somewhere that felt less benign; somewhere he could cheerfully uncover a nest of spies and feel that all was right with the world.

Leo took a packet of cigarettes from his coat pocket and held it out for Sommers to take one before helping himself. He had his lighter out of his other pocket before Sommers could reach his own, and when he leaned in to light the other man's cigarette, he smelled hard soap and something like fresh air. He stayed there a second too long, in case he hadn't made his intentions utterly clear by now. He watched Sommers' throat work as he swallowed.

"That's Marston." Sommers took a puff from his cigarette and blew the smoke out toward the ceiling. It took Leo an instant to remember that he had asked about the bearded man. "He's staying in the old gamekeeper's cottage at Little Briars."

The dossier hadn't had anything on Marston, and if Templeton's people couldn't find anything out about a person it was because they didn't exist or were using an assumed name. So Leo made up his mind to talk to this Marston fellow tomorrow. The man had come to the victim's funeral, so he couldn't be an outsider even if he wasn't talking to anyone, and even if Sommers said he was only "staying" at the cottage.

Now that he pretty much had the lay of the land, it was time to go before anyone wondered why he was more curious about the inhabitants of Wychcomb St. Mary's than about its windows.

"I'm for bed," Leo said. "I suppose I'll see you—"

"Wait." Sommers' hand wrapped around Leo's arm, inches away from where that bullet had been. Leo could feel the strength and heat of it through the tweed of the secondhand coat he had bought for this role. "You didn't ask about Wendy."

"Pardon?" Leo hadn't asked about Wendy Smythe because he had been able to identify her instantly as the overgrown schoolgirl who was half asleep in an armchair, one of the Griffiths children tugging at her untidy black plait. He knew she had been billeted with Miss Delacourt and Miss Pickering at Little Briars after being evacuated from London at the start of the war and had somehow never left.

"You asked about everyone else, but you didn't ask about Wendy," Dr. Sommers explained. "I thought it might have been an oversight."

For a moment Leo had no idea if he were being accused of nosiness or espionage, or—given how Sommers' hand lingered on Leo's sleeve longer than it needed to—if he were being picked up. He decided his purposes would be best served by assuming it had been the last. "You've caught me out, Dr. Sommers," he said confidingly, leaning into the doctor's space. "I can't mind my own business. It's a character flaw."

They were close enough that Leo could hear Sommers' breath hitch. They stayed like that for a moment, about as close as two gentlemen could be in a vicarage parlor.

Then Sommers' hand dropped. "Goodnight, Mr. Page." His voice was low, pitched loud enough for only Leo to hear, and it seemed to hold both an invitation and a threat.

"I'm staying at the Rising Sun," Leo said before slipping from the room. He didn't think the doctor would make use of that information—not yet at least—but he wanted to make his interests crystal clear.

As Leo walked down the high street toward the inn, he gave it seven to three odds that he'd find his way into the doctor's bed in less than a week. Ten to one odds that he'd solve the crime and have it nicely covered up in that same period of time. And then he'd get back on the train to London. He'd be none the worse for his time in Wychcomb St. Mary, no matter how much havoc he wreaked while he was there.

Chapter 3

J ames rapped on the cottage door. There was no answer, but then Marston never did answer on the first knock. James rapped again, harder this time. "It's dashed cold, Marston. Might we cut the ritual short today?"

There was a beat. "I'm in the garden."

James followed the dirt path around to the back of the cottage. Marston, wearing his old army coat and a wool cap that had seen better days, was fiddling with a box that James knew held one of his beehives. With his woolen cap pulled low over his forehead and his beard covering the lower part of his face, only his eyes—haunted and wary—were visible.

"Is there much you have to do with them in the winter?" James asked. "The bees, I mean? I thought they just sort of slept."

"Why do you keep coming here?" Marston didn't look up from the wooden box. "I'm not one of your patients."

James wasn't quite certain where Marston came from or who his people were. He always managed to look thoroughly disreputable, but every now and then, James thought he could hear the remnants of a very expensive accent in the man's rough voice.

"Is there a rule about doctors only being allowed to speak with their patients?" James asked lightly. He stepped closer, as cautiously as he would approach a strange dog. "I'm here as a neighbor."

Marston snorted. "You're here on suicide watch," he muttered, which was the third complete sentence he had uttered today, an accomplishment that had to be counted as monumental progress.

"I'm really not," James said. "But should I be?" Marston had drunk himself into a stupor a few times during the year he had lived in the gamekeeper's cottage, and it had crossed James's mind that this might be a slow form of suicide, but he didn't think it was. Marston didn't seem depressed so much as angry, which was all too reasonable a reaction to what he had been through.

"No, damn you," Marston growled.

James was counting that as a fourth sentence, a personal best. Usually, Marston glared and grunted while James kept up a one-sided conversation. "I'm here because you're a hermit and I worry you might forget how to act around people or how to talk."

"How to talk?"

"Right. Talking. It's making words with your face." James thought he could see the beginnings of a smile beneath that shaggy beard, so he decided to press on. "It was kind of you to go to Mrs. Hoggett's funeral."

Marston said nothing.

"I hadn't realized you and she were friendly," James said.

Marston spoke without looking up from the slat he was fixing in place. "We weren't."

"Oh, it's just that you're so committed to the social niceties that you attend funerals and tea parties as a matter of obligation."

"No, that's you, Sommers."

It was meant as an insult, but it still counted as another sentence, and anyway, Marston was right about James's fondness for the niceties. These days he'd take any and every reminder that people were capable of something other than reducing one another to piles of meat. Tea parties, dull chats with the vicar, and the rote routines of village life tethered him to a world that too often seemed to slip out of existence. Mrs. Hoggett's death had made that tether even flimsier than it had been before.

Marston glared at James. "I'm going to tell you this so you'll go away and leave me in peace. And it's exactly what I told the constable. I hardly knew Mrs. Hoggett. When the weather was fine, she'd sometimes wave or call hello as she walked to work at Wych Hall."

The footpath through the wood between Little Briars and the hall passed directly in front of Marston's cottage. The cottage was owned by Edith Pickering and was situated on the farthest reaches of her property, where it abutted Colonel Armstrong's land. The path itself was an easement or a right of way or some such thing and the subject of generational disputes between the Pickerings and the Armstrongs. The latest chapter in the saga occurred some years before the war when Colonel Armstrong had tried to block access to his end of the footpath, which emptied out, he claimed, inconveniently close to the terrace of his own house. This attempt hadn't endeared him to his tenants, several of whom used the path as a shortcut to and from the village. In the end, Edith's solicitor had needed to take quite a firm hand with the colonel to remind him that he had no control over the path, however close it passed to his house.

"The night she died, Mrs. Hoggett went to Wych Hall at six o'clock to help in the kitchen during the colonel's dinner party," James said.

"I don't know anything about that. I didn't see anyone or anything that night."

The trouble with beards, James thought, was that they made it so hard to tell when a man was lying.

"Anyway," Marston went on, "I went to the funeral not for her, but for the girl."

It took James a moment to understand what Marston was saying. "For Wendy?"

"She brings me eggs when she has them. And I give her honey when I have any. And then she goes on her way," he added pointedly, with a look toward the path as if he could will James to walk out the way he had come.

"Well. That really was kind of you then."

"Sod *off*, will you, Sommers."

James held up his hands in surrender and took several steps backward—colliding into a hard, solid body. He whipped around to see Mr. Page.

"I'm counting to three, and you're both getting the fuck out of my sight." Marston's fists were clenched. "One."

James grabbed Mr. Page's arm and tugged him out of the garden toward the front of the cottage.

"I was going for a walk and I heard voices," Mr. Page said affably. "Thought I'd pop in."

"Save it." James pulled Mr. Page down the footpath until Marston could no longer see or hear them. He kept his grip hard on Page's arm, partly because he was annoyed that Page had disturbed Marston, partly because he had been having something like a conversation with Marston before Page interrupted. Certainly, it was only a coincidence that his fingers, of their own volition, seemed to want to seek out the feel of lean, ropy muscle beneath the tweed of Page's coat.

"Everyone's terribly grumpy this morning," Page said when they stopped walking.

"I suppose now you're going to tell me you needed to interview Marston because you're writing a pamphlet on beekeeping."

There was a spark of amusement in Page's dark eyes. "Of course not. That would be silly. I'm writing a treatise on—"

"On church windows or some such rot. Despite the fact that you'd never heard of our three hares window." That had kept James up into the small hours of the morning. He knew he had seen Page before, and he knew Page wasn't here about church architecture or stone tracery or anything of the sort. Once he took those two facts as proven, it didn't take long for James to arrive at the unpleasant truth.

"You know," Page said conversationally, "this is the second time you've grabbed my arm like that." He glanced down at James's hand. "I'm beginning to think you like touching me."

"I'll do more than grab you if you pester Marston again." But he didn't let go of Page's arm. Instead, he tightened his grip experimentally.

A slow smile spread across Page's mouth. "Promises, promises."

"Oh, for heaven's sake. You're going to get yourself thrashed if you talk to men like that."

"Not by you, I don't think." Page leaned back against the trunk of an oak tree so he had to look up at James to meet his eye. They were about the same height and size, but Page was deliberately making himself small and unintimidating, as if he were trying to put James at his ease.

"No, not by me," James conceded, letting his hand drop to his side. "Listen, Page, I don't know who you are or why you're in Wychcomb St. Mary, but I do know you aren't writing about church windows, and I'm fairly certain I took a bullet out of your arm in a room above an abandoned charcuterie in Caen." James had been whisked away from the field hospital without any explanation beyond vague mentions of a patient who couldn't be moved. When James arrived, he had found a man near delirious with infection. He wore, not an army uniform, but the battered clothes of a French Maquis. It was hardly the first time James had treated a member of the French resistance during those weeks after the arrival of allied troops into Normandy, but by the looks of the wound on this man's arm, he had been shot before Operation Overlord, and had simply let the wound fester until he collapsed from illness. James had done the best he could with minimal supplies and in a setting that was about as far removed from a sterile operating theater as could be imagined.

"I bet if I rolled up your sleeve I'd see the scar," James continued. "Two inches long at least, crescent-shaped, about halfway between the elbow and shoulder on the front of the arm, matching exit wound." During the war, James had assumed that the details of various injuries—body parts stitched together or lopped off; knife wounds, bullet wounds, burns—would fade into a manageable confusion of memories. Instead, he could recall all too much of it in gruesome detail. He had long since given up hope that he'd ever forget, and now merely hoped that he might one day tolerate sharing his mind with this catalogue of horrors.

Page looked up at him from beneath a fringe of dark lashes. "I'm flattered that you want to undress me."

James snorted, his morose train of thought interrupted by the man's shameless flirtation. "You don't deny it."

"No, because when I take you to bed you'll see any and all of my scars for yourself. Yours was the most neatly done, however. I'm certain I'll find a way to thank you."

"That's what you're thinking of right now?" James sputtered. "Not that I'm accusing you of being some kind of intelligence agent?"

"You don't seem terribly worried about whatever it is I might be," Page said, his eyes wide with feigned innocence, "so I suppose I'm not either. Now, onto the part where—"

"No, I'm not worried. When Scotland Yard's sudden lack of interest in a suspicious death coincides with the arrival of a man on false pretenses, a man who has some connection with, I'm guessing, Special Branch, then no, I'm not worried." All James cared about was for life in Wychcomb St. Mary to return to normal as soon as possible. Intelligence officers, by their very nature, didn't advertise their doings, which meant Page wouldn't get in the way of James's continued efforts to convince himself that nothing was amiss. He cleared his throat and tried to sound calm. "I don't care what brings somebody like you to investigate her death," he said, "but please don't pester Marston. He's been through enough." They had all been through enough. The whole world had been through enough, and it was high time to get down to the business of being quiet and ordinary. People like Leo Page, people whose entire reason for being was rooting around in darkness and danger, had no part in that. "Just do your job, and the sooner you leave, the better."

IT WAS ADORABLE THAT Sommers thought he was involved with anything as straightforward as Special Branch. Leo was almost touched by the man's innocence. He didn't run across much of that these days. Really, the man was just precious, the way his broad shoulders squared up and his affable face got all serious and fierce when he wanted to protect his friends, the way he didn't hesitate to lay hands on Leo but kept his touch far too light to do any harm.

After reluctantly leaving the doctor in the woods—it was cold but not so cold that they couldn't have found some way to divert themselves—Leo wrapped his coat more tightly around his chest and made his way back down the path. There were footprints in the soil that didn't belong to either him or Sommers. There were also several ruts caused by bicycle wheels.

The footpath forked when it approached the village, one branch heading to the high street and the other, having dwindled to the merest scratch in the ground, led to the garden gate at the vicarage. There Leo found Mrs. Griffiths, the vicar's wife, scattering seeds on the cold ground for a few drab brown birds.

If Leo had thought Mrs. Griffiths had been shabbily dressed at the funeral, he now saw the error of his ways. The out of fashion but serviceable black frock she had on yesterday might well have been her finery if today's threadbare and ill-fitting tweed skirt and moth-eaten jumper were her everyday wear. She wore no hat, but a muffler that covered half her head and did nothing to obscure the fact that she was badly in need of a trip to the hairdresser. Either that, or she ought to make peace with not doing anything with that mass of unruly-looking dark curls and resign herself to putting it in a knot. She saw him approach and waved, causing seeds to fly out of her hand to the great confusion of the birds on the ground.

"Mr. Page! Out for a stroll? I've resolved to stay out of Daniel's way while he's meeting with the Sunday school teachers, so I came out here to feed these poor wretches."

The sparrows at her feet milled about, picking through the seeds until they found the sort they wanted. Leo had once known an old man who had gone outside every morning all winter with a palm full of seeds; by March he had bramblings and chaffinches eating out of his hand. By May he had been shot dead by a sniper, but that wasn't the point of the story. The point was that in the unlikely event that Leo ever grew old, perhaps he'd devote himself to feeding birds by hand like some kind of good witch.

"May I?" he asked, holding out his hand for some birdseed.

"By all means. I know one isn't supposed to feed birds because it upsets the natural order of things, or something to that effect. It interferes with migration, I think. Could that be it? Or is it survival of the fittest, perhaps? Daniel read me something from one of the papers he takes, but I can't remember."

Leo, who had never once in his life thought about the ethics of feeding birds, and tried his best never to think of the ethics of anything, murmured something he hoped Mrs. Griffiths would interpret as she saw fit. He crouched down with his hand out, but the birds scattered as he moved.

"But the truth is," Mrs. Griffiths went on, haphazardly scattering another handful of seeds onto the dirt, "I'm not sure there is a natural order of things anymore. I'm quite sure a good number of birds died during the war, don't you think? So, really, how can it matter whether I feed these little fellows or not?"

This observation comported so thoroughly with Leo's own worldview that he felt in perfect charity with the vicar's wife. He returned to his feet and regarded her with new approval. "Cigarette?" he asked, producing the packet from his coat. From the way she was babbling with little prompting on his part, he guessed she was starved for conversation, and that it would take no effort to have her divulge anything she knew about the night of the murder.

"Oh, bless you," she said, taking a cigarette and leaning forward for him to light it. "We can sit here, if you dare." She gestured to what had once been a bench but was now a collection of half-rotten boards.

"I live dangerously," he said, which was no less than the truth. The bench creaked ominously but seemed able to support them both. "How long have you lived here?"

"Going on eight years. The place was falling apart when Daniel was sent here, and this is such a tiny parish that there isn't the money to fix it up. Heaven knows we can't do anything about it ourselves, not with the children's school fees and everything else." Leo suspected that she was in the habit of apologizing for the state of her house. "The vicar who had this post before us didn't keep it up either, I'm afraid, so the poor shambles is going on four decades of neglect. Reverend Sommers must have been eighty when he finally died. I can hardly blame him for letting the roof leak." She sighed. "And for letting the plumbing go to ruin." She fell silent, as if in mourning for the plumbing.

"That would be Dr. Sommers' uncle? Odd for a child to be sent to live with an elderly bachelor uncle." He spoke in an off-hand way that suggested he didn't much care about Dr. Sommers either personally or professionally but was just trying to engage a woman in conversation.

She nodded. "The usual thing. Mother in the colonies, child sent to England to be educated and passed around amongst relations during the holidays."

There was a hint of flatness in Mrs. Griffiths' accent. She was perhaps Australian or South African, but had lived in England long enough to acquire most of the usual vowels. "I saw the doctor this morning on my walk," Leo said. "And also a Mr. Marston, I think his name was? I'm afraid I startled him and, well, he might have taken it amiss."

"Oh, dear. Did he snap at you? You can't hold it against him. He had a bad war. He was skin and bones when he came here, and he never speaks of his people. I'm not sure if they died or if..." She let her voice trail off, as if realizing she was spilling secrets that weren't her own. "In any event," she said more briskly, "you can't blame him for being a bit jumpy. Lord knows I go a bit daft when I have to take a mouse out of a trap, so it's no wonder men can get strange after all that killing." She scattered another handful of seeds, even though the birds, having gorged themselves, seemed to have lost interest. Leo remained silent, hoping Mrs. Griffiths would talk more about Mr. Marston.

"Dr. Sommers' father was another one. A shell shock case, I mean," the vicar's wife continued. "Or, battle fatigue, I suppose we're calling it now. Of course, I never knew the man, but he took his own life and then his wife ran off to India. Or maybe it was the other way around. Things do get jumbled in the retelling."

"I haven't even been here for two days and I've already heard half a dozen versions of how the charwoman died," Leo said casually, pausing to take a drag from his cigarette.

"They'll never stop talking about it," Mrs. Griffiths said. "They run out of things to talk about in a village, so they run through the same gossip again and again. Every unfortunate thing one's ever done gets talked to death." The vehemence in her tone made Leo wonder whether she spoke from experience. "I suppose one can't blame them. One does get bored in a place like this." She took a final puff on her cigarette and then dropped it to the ground where she crushed it with a badly scuffed boot.

A shadow fell on the ground before them, and when Leo looked up, he saw Colonel Armstrong's fair-haired secretary approaching from the same garden gate through which Leo had entered a few minutes earlier. He wore an unremarkable dark hat and blandly nondescript tweed coat, as if trying to subdue his good looks. If so, he had failed. In the colorless, derelict garden, he was like a bird of paradise among the sparrows.

"They're certainly talking about poor Mrs. Hoggett now," the secretary said. "I had to mail a letter, and everyone at the post office was talking about how much Veronal had been found in her system. *System* sounds horribly euphemistic."

Mrs. Griffiths seemed to remember that introductions were required of her. "Edward, this is Mr. Page. Mr. Page, Mr.

Norris," she said, unhooking the spectacles from her collar and perching them on her nose, as if to get a better look at the visitor. "You look very fine for a trip to the post office. Why are my glasses always smudged?" she asked, seemingly to nobody in particular. She dug a handkerchief out of her pocket to wipe the lenses, but two other handkerchiefs came tumbling out. Leo bent to retrieve them, and saw that Mrs. Griffiths' careless style of dress extended to her handkerchiefs—they were made of plain cotton, threadbare, embroidered with what he assumed to be the initials of her maiden name: M.O. Given that her children appeared to be school age, the lady was highly overdue for a purchase of new handkerchiefs.

Leo stood and tipped the brim of his hat at the secretary. "The girl at the Rising Sun said you were both there the night she died. Must have been a dreadful shock."

"Oh, yes," Mrs. Griffiths said unconvincingly before shaking her head and sighing. "If I'm honest, she was just the sort of woman one expects to be murdered."

"Mary," Mr. Norris reproved.

"Well, it's true. I've lost count of all the tales I've heard from the old cats in this village. As if there's something I could do about it."

"What kind of tales?" Leo asked.

"She had a habit of poking her nose into things, I'm afraid."

Leo didn't like that one bit. It was his professional opinion that all you had to do was scratch a snoop and find a blackmailer, and blackmail complicated matters dreadfully.

"I can tell you, there's nothing worth prying into at the hall," Norris said. "Dullest post I've ever had. But the village does have its attractions." He didn't even try to conceal the fact that these words were directed at the vicar's wife, but the lady seemed oblivious.

"The cook at the hall is very good," Mrs. Griffiths said. "She manages to do marvelous things, even with rationing being what it is. A couple of turnips and some dried beef and she'll have you eating like a king."

Leo did not miss the way Norris rolled his eyes. The fellow had evidently come for a flirtation and was being rebuffed in favor of discussing the virtues of turnips.

Up close, there was no question but that Mary Griffiths was a very pretty woman. She was about his age, which was to say nearing thirty. He had at first thought her a good ten years older, closer to her husband's age. Her particular style of bad dressing—a smudged pair of spectacles hanging from the collar of a badly darned jumper, a pencil tucked behind her ear, that *hair*—was the sort that transcended age. He might have thought Mrs. Griffiths was the stepmother of the children who had been present at the funeral, but the little girl looked so much like her mother that they had to be related. This likely meant Mrs. Griffiths had been married at about twenty, and at that age, she must have been a beauty.

Nevertheless, she had married an older clergyman. Did she ever wonder what the girl she had been must think of the life she led now, tossed outside while her much older husband met with Sunday school teachers? He thought briefly of Dorothea Brooke, who last night had married that decrepit old man despite Leo's sternly telling his copy of *Middlemarch* that it was a bad idea. Not that Griffiths was in any way decrepit. But Leo could see how Norris might think it safe to assume that the pretty young wife of an older man might be up for a flirtation, or even more. Maybe she was. Maybe Mrs. Hoggett had found out.

He was searching for loose threads, anything he could pull on in order to unravel this mess of fabric. It might not lead him to the murderer, but it would lead him somewhere.

"The colonel must entertain often if he has such a good cook," Leo suggested. He was coming sideways at the question he really wanted to ask, which was why the colonel had held the dinner party in the first place.

"No, not often. Occasionally he dines with people he knew from the war or his family's business," Norris said. "But never anything grand."

Mrs. Griffiths muttered something that sounded like "skinflint."

"But the evening of Mrs. Hoggett's death, all the guests were people from the village, weren't they?"

"He does that from time to time," Mrs. Griffiths said. "He invites all the local eminences at once so as to discharge his social obligations for the quarter, I daresay. It's usually the same group. Miss Pickering and Miss Delacourt are his neighbors, and they brought Wendy, naturally. James—that's Dr. Sommers—went because he's a darling dear and goes to all these terrible things. He was called away to a patient before we sat down to dine, though. And Edward was there, of course," she said, gesturing at the secretary.

"It's too awkward not to ask me to dine when there's company," the secretary said with a tone that was not quite a complaint. "And I evened out the numbers of men and women."

"In the taproom I heard someone say they thought the charwoman might have been killed by accident," Leo lied. "That maybe one of the guests was the intended victim."

"Oh, everybody's taken to amateur sleuthing," Mrs. Griffiths said dismissively. "You wouldn't believe the theories I've heard. Besides, it makes no sense." She tapped her cigarette onto the bare earth. "How do you push the wrong person down the stairs? Or is the idea that the Veronal was intended for somebody else, and Mrs. Hoggett got it by mistake, and toppled down the stairs on her own? That could be. Mrs. Hoggett was just the type of servant to drink from a glass after clearing the table, I'm afraid."

"Whose glass?" Leo asked. He knew that the police laboratory had examined all the glasses and dishes, and no traces of Veronal or any other suspicious substance had been found in any of them. But he wanted to hear all about the village's most secret enmities.

"The colonel," Mrs. Griffiths said at once.

"Mary," Norris said reproachfully.

"Why would someone want to kill Colonel Armstrong?" Leo asked innocently. "I thought you said he was perfectly boring." He directed this last remark at the secretary.

Norris and Mrs. Griffiths stared at him and then glanced at one another. "Mr. Page," Mrs. Griffiths said, "have you ever met a rich man somebody *didn't* want to kill?"

Chapter 4

J ames checked his watch. He had an hour left before his evening patients would be waiting for him at the surgery, which was just enough time for a cup of tea at Little Briars. The Murphy boy was recovering from tonsillitis, an ointment had been prescribed for the postman's chilblains, and the district nurse was cleaning a gash a farm laborer had gotten on her leg. There was not a single interesting or troubling case on his roster of patients, thank God.

As he walked up the drive, he saw Edith Pickering's solicitor leaving the house. "Good evening, Henry," James called.

"Damned freezing," Henry responded, turning up the collar of his coat as he walked briskly to his car. "Stay warm, Sommers."

It was unquestionably cold, but James hardly felt it. He had been walking nearly all day, visiting patients. Well, visiting patients and arguing with Special Branch agents in the woods. The memory unsettled him. Damn near everything unsettled him these days, which was the problem with having a brain that stubbornly refused to grasp that the war was over. Leo Page seemed like the living embodiment of a war that still roiled on in the dark recesses of James's mind. That night in Caen, he had been certain he was stitching up a French freedom fighter, but at the vicarage, he had been equally certain Page was a mild-mannered clerk with a too-obvious taste for men. This juxtaposition left him feeling disoriented, as if the battlefields of France were encroaching into his village. The rustle of wind and the scent of hearth fire seemed to transform into the distant sounds of shellfire, the odor of gunpowder lingering on corpses—

He knocked on the heavy oak door of Little Briars, fighting the urge to press his face against it as a reminder that he was safe, he was home. Within seconds the door was thrown open by Wendy. "Hullo James. I'm an heiress," she said. Her tone was light, but she had the bleak, unfocused look he was used to seeing on survivors of air raids.

"Pardon?"

"Mrs. Hoggett left it all to me."

"How much money can she possibly have had?" She was a charwoman, for heaven's sake.

"She said she had a bit put aside, but I didn't know it was that much. Nearly a thousand pounds, which may not seem a lot to you, but I've never had any money at all, so I feel quite rich."

People had been killed for less, James reflected, and then felt guilty for having formed the thought. Wendy must have guessed the turn of his mind, because she scowled. "It was a nasty trick for her to play, because now everybody's going to think I did her in."

"Nobody's going to think anything of the sort," James said automatically. He steered Wendy toward the parlor, where Cora and Edith shared the settee nearest to the fire. Edith was attacking her knitting with her customary fury while Cora absently stroked a ball of wool. The room was almost uncomfortably warm, and James had to peel off coat, muffler, hat, and gloves before sitting.

After the women had filled him in on the contents of Mrs. Hoggett's will ("a single page," Edith had said, jabbing a needle into the wool, "but Henry said it'll stand."), the four of them sat in stunned speechlessness.

"I can't imagine where she came by it," Edith said, her lips pursed in a way that suggested that she did not think the money could have been acquired by fair means.

"Wasn't she an old servant of yours?" James asked. He did not miss the glance the two older ladies darted at one another. Before he could press the point, Wendy interrupted.

"What I can't imagine is why she left it to me. Unless it was pity," the girl said in a small voice, breaking the silence. Before anyone could protest, she hastily got to her feet and headed for the door. "I really ought to go feed the chickens." A moment later they heard the back door slam and the chickens squawking.

"We've told her again and again that she's welcome to stay with us as long as she likes," Cora said. "Or for good. We're fond of the girl." There was an unspoken *even if she is a bit odd* at the end of Cora's statement.

"She's at that age," Edith said. "You can't say anything to please them."

James thought Wendy was simply grieving—maybe not for the unpleasant Mrs. Hoggett, but in a more general sense. She had lost a mother and presumably a father before that, so this recent loss might brush the cobwebs off some old sorrow. James's own parents had died when he was a child, and he had often wondered if that was why death took him badly. He ought to have developed a callus over whatever part of his heart was meant for mourning, but instead, it was like a wound that never quite healed.

He took his leave. There was no sign of Wendy by the chicken coop or in the kitchen garden. She was probably traipsing about in the dark, which James didn't care for at all. As he walked back to the village, he decided that the more he thought about it, the less he liked what Wendy had said about people suspecting she murdered Mrs. Hoggett for her money. Because she was right—people would speculate, again and again, until it took on the force of truth. After all, she was at that blasted dinner party. Wendy had always been a bit odd, they'd say, and it would be true. For the hundredth time, James cursed the Lewis baby for having chosen to be born that night; otherwise, he would have been at Wych Hall and might have seen what really happened.

The only way to stop that false story from being bandied about was to find out the truth behind Mrs. Hoggett's death. He recoiled almost bodily from the prospect. Discovering the truth would mean an end to his grand plan of pretending it hadn't happened. But he would do what it took to protect Wendy. She had nobody in this world besides a pair of elderly spinsters. James knew what it was like to be alone and adrift. So he set his jaw and headed toward the pub. As he walked, a chill that had nothing to do with the weather passed through him.

WHEN THE DOOR TO THE taproom of the Rising Sun swung open, letting in a gust of icy air, Leo wasn't entirely surprised to see Dr. Sommers. This was a small village, after all. But he was surprised indeed when Sommers scanned the room and headed directly for Leo's table. This was rather more forward behavior than Leo had expected from the doctor.

"May I..." The doctor bit his lip. "May I join you?"

"Please," Leo said, gesturing to the empty chair across from him.

"What have you learned?" Sommers asked, pulling out the chair and sitting.

So Sommers meant for this to be a business visit. Too bad for him. "Well." Leo removed a small notepad from his breast pocket. "I've learned you go to London two days a week, and that nobody knows why. You take the early train and return by tea. Two of the doctors from Fladbury are on call when you're away, and in exchange, you refer nearly all your surgical cases to them." He kept his voice low enough that he couldn't be overheard. "I might make a fair guess as to what secretive activities a man such as yourself might pursue in London, but two days a week seems excessive." He brought his mug to his mouth and regarded Sommers over the rim. "Always the quiet ones, I suppose."

Sommers blinked. "That's what you've been doing with your day? Asking about me?"

"Well, no, of course not. I've been soaking up all the best—which is to say the seediest—village gossip. You'd be shocked to know what people will tell a perfect stranger. I've learned which nefarious characters everyone suspects of ration fraud and adultery and just about every crime other than murder. Wychcomb St. Mary is a sink of vice, I'm sorry to say." The barmaid put a pint of brown ale before Sommers, and Leo wondered what it must be like to live in a place where your drinking preferences were known before you spoke. "But let's put that aside because at the moment, The Mystery of the Brilliant Young Surgeon is rather more interesting to me than all the dead charwomen in all the kingdom."

Sommers paused, his mug halfway to his lips. "Brilliant young surgeon? Rubbish."

"I don't think it is." For one, there was no possibility that a mediocre surgeon would have been brought in to stitch up his shooting arm, which was also his forging arm, and in general, a very useful arm for the empire to have intact. "I'd really like to know what you're doing in a tiny village rather than cutting people up for science and profit or what have you."

Leo wasn't trying to be polite, or sensitive, or even a decent person. Sometimes finding out the truth meant being an utter bastard. But he hadn't expected Sommers to turn ashen, hadn't expected the doctor's hands to shake, causing some ale to slosh over the side of his glass, spilling onto the table. Leo gently took the mug from the doctor's hands and mopped up the ale with his own handkerchief. He didn't know exactly what he had said to cause that reaction, and it might simply have been the man's regrets about wasted potential, but he was filing this episode away for later reference. For now, he thought a tactful silence more likely to gain the doctor's confidence.

"What else did you learn?" Sommers asked after he recovered himself.

"Mr. Norris, the secretary, is generally considered a local treasure. Agnes, behind the bar, says that he" –here Leo made a show of paging through his notes to read the exact words— "smells like an advertisement." He looked up to see that Sommers was smiling despite himself. "And Agnes also has it on good authority that Colonel Armstrong pays this secretary only half what some other fellow pays his own secretary."

"Is that so?" Sommers frowned. "I wouldn't have thought Armstrong the type to hire a cut-rate secretary, nor would I have thought the work he offered exciting enough to make a man settle for lower wages."

If Agnes's source was to be trusted, then the matter of the underpaid secretary was another loose thread for Leo to pull at. It could be as simple as Norris taking a reduced wage because he wanted access to Armstrong's papers in order to sell secrets. Or it could be that Norris had something in his past that hindered his chances of finding better employment. "Agnes seems to believe that Mr. Norris takes this pitiful wage out of civic duty, to counterbalance the dearth of handsome men in Wychcomb St. Mary."

"I take that very personally," Sommers said with mock affront.

"Oh, but you shouldn't," Leo said, all reassurance. "Your name came up. She said you were pleasant to look at, but one can't develop an appropriate pash—her word, not mine, I assure you—for the man who lances one's boils."

The doctor's shoulders shook and he buried his head in his hands. "I'm quite crushed," he said when his laughter subsided.

"Yes, well, she told me that I don't seem like the marrying kind, just like her bachelor uncle. You may have guessed that Agnes is quite correct on that count."

"Agnes's uncle had a pet monkey," Sommers sputtered.

Now Leo was laughing. He couldn't remember the last time he'd laughed this hard, great sobs of laughter shuddering through his body. When he looked across the table at Sommers, he saw the man wiping tears of laughter from his eyes. Leo slid his foot under the table until it brushed the doctor's.

"So, what *do* you do in London two days a week, Dr. Sommers? It can't be entirely in the pursuit of vice."

Sommers pulled his foot away from Leo's. "We're not talking about that."

"Why not? The movements of suspects are always of interest to investigators."

Sommers raised his eyebrows. "I'm not a suspect. I was at a lying in the night Mrs. Hoggett died, in plain view of the district nurse, the laboring mother, and Colonel Armstrong's housekeeper."

"You're a doctor. You could have prescribed the woman an excessive dose of barbiturate."

"And then wished upon a falling star that she tripped down a convenient flight of stairs? Don't be silly. And why would I have done that in the first place?"

Leo was glad that Sommers seemed unconcerned to learn that he wasn't above suspicion. "The motive is almost always money. It's tedious, if I'm honest. In crimes of passion the motive might be jealousy or anger or revenge, but for anything premeditated, it's money or secrets." He didn't for a minute think that Sommers was mixed up in the death of Mildred Hoggett. The culprit had to have been on hand to hit her on the head or push her down the stairs. But Leo's usual practice was to dig up everything that could possibly be uncovered. Secrets were like a vein of ore; tiny little strands might lead to a mother lode. He was going to have to look into what Sommers did on his jaunts to London. Hell, he was going to have to look into a number of things this man wouldn't approve of.

"About the money." Sommers filled Leo in on the contents of Mildred Hoggett's will.

Leo whistled. "All to Wendy Smythe." He hadn't seen that coming. Hadn't expected the woman to have a will, for that matter.

"Every last shilling," Sommers said.

"Where'd she come by that sort of money?" Leo mused aloud. Scratch a snoop and find a blackmailer, he repeated to himself.

The doctor shifted in his seat. "She seemed to have a habit of poking into things that weren't her business. I caught her looking into the patient files in my surgery."

Well, well. He hadn't expected Sommers to cooperate. And indeed, the man looked like he had just taken a bite of spoiled meat.

"And," Sommers went on, his cheeks reddening. "She also went through my cupboards upstairs. I only hired her to clean the downstairs rooms and the surgery. She had no business being upstairs."

It took Leo embarrassingly long—a second or more—to realize why the doctor was blushing. "A sensible practice. That way you can entertain visitors upstairs without worrying about anyone coming across the evidence."

The doctor was beet red now, all the way from his cheekbones to the collar of his shirt. "There's no evidence," he hissed. "There's no entertaining, either. Good God, man. You are horribly indiscreet for a...whatever you are."

"I know," Leo said cheerfully. "It's part of my charm." It was part of his strategy, but he wasn't going to explain that. "So, she could have been snooping because she was a blackmailer. Or she could have been looking for things to steal. Either way, she could have amassed a tidy sum, especially if she had been doing so for many years. Did anyone know about the will?"

"I'd swear that nobody at Little Briars did." And then, as if remembering who he was talking to, his body stiffened. "Although I don't suppose you'll take my word for it."

Indeed, Leo would not. He wasn't in the habit of taking anybody's word for anything, especially statements made to protect a friend. Instead of answering, he pushed his pack of cigarettes across the table for Sommers to take one. "So, that's why you're here, willing to cooperate with my wicked schemes," he said lightly. "You want to make sure nobody pins this on the girl." Even less than a thousand pounds could mean a lot to a girl who, by all accounts, didn't have a penny to bless herself with.

Sommers frowned. "In a matter of speaking, yes." He took a cigarette, casting it a glance as if it might be some kind of nefarious trick. "A necessary evil," he added, his jaw tight.

Leo hadn't known he was capable of having his feelings hurt. It had been so long since he cared one way or another about what anyone thought of him that the awareness of wounded vanity returned to him like the prickling sensation of a limb too long unused. He was so accustomed to playing a role, acting a part, completing a mission, that sometimes he found it convenient to ignore that beneath the mission there was a man. Maybe it was the fact that he was in England, his nominal home; maybe it was the fact that he was using his own name. But whatever the reason, he found it difficult at this moment to think of himself as an agent, as a tool. He looked across the table and wished Sommers didn't look so utterly sickened by the prospect of dealing with him. Leo was conscious that this was a lapse on his own part. It was perfectly reasonable of Sommers not to relish the prospect of having Leo around. After all, Leo would peel back layer after layer until all the village's sins and weaknesses were laid before him, including the doctor's own. But finding out the truth wasn't the goal—the truth was just another weapon, a knife to put in the right person's hand, a grenade waiting to explode.

"That's me, all right," Leo remarked, flicking open his lighter and lighting both their cigarettes behind his cupped hand. "A necessary evil."

Chapter 5

At this rate, everyone in the village was going to get tonsillitis. Both the Griffiths children were tucked in bed in the drafty vicarage nursery, and James had seen four patients at morning surgery with the same symptoms.

"You can give them broth if they'll take it," James told an especially ragged looking Mary Griffiths. "Or some elderberry syrup. If you haven't any, then Mrs. Clemens at Wych Hall might be able to scare some up." The colonel's housekeeper had a way of making things appear even when all the shops were out of stock; James chose not to inquire too closely into her means.

"I can't stand beef tea," Polly Griffiths complained from her bed, her voice scratchy and weak. "I'd rather die."

"Hush," Mary admonished her daughter. "You're not meant to talk."

Something about the little girl languishing theatrically in her bed reminded him of Wendy when she had first come to the village. She had always had a flair for the dramatic and hadn't been much older than Polly and Owen Griffiths at the time. During holidays from university and leave during the war he had seen her grow from a gangly child to a—well, still frankly gangly—young woman.

James dropped his thermometer into his bag and snapped it shut. "You're going to fall ill yourself if you don't get some rest," he told the vicar's wife.

"Rest? Fat chance of that happening," she scoffed. He followed her down the stairs and into the kitchen, where the breakfast dishes still sat piled in the sink.

"Ask Wendy to help. You know she loves the children." He had nearly said that she loved being useful, which was nothing more or less than the truth. She was always delivering bundles of kindling to some of the poorer families and pots of quince jam to elderly ladies. He wondered if her efforts to be useful had arisen from wanting to feel like she belonged in the village that was her adopted home. Did she fear that Edith would throw her out on her ear if she didn't earn her keep? Edith herself had said that she offered the girl a permanent home under no uncertain terms, but Wendy might have doubted that they really wanted her. James knew something of how it felt not to know if one was a wanted family member or simply a burden.

"I can hardly ask her to be an unpaid nursery maid," Mary said, bringing James back to the present. "It's my own fault for not knowing what I'm doing here." She gestured around the untidy kitchen. "I grew up in poky little flats until my mother brought us back to England. Then she married my stepfather and we lived in squalid hotels. I don't know how to do things properly—not keeping a house, not raising the twins—"

"Don't talk about my friend like that. Your children are lovely. Your home is..." As he struggled to find a word, a large hound bounded into the kitchen, put his feet on the edge of the sink, and began enthusiastically licking the breakfast dishes. "Homelike," he announced, proud of himself for having settled on a word that was both true and somewhat complimentary. "It's all right to ask for help, you know."

She shot him a shrewd look. "You first."

He held his hands up in surrender. "I know, I know. I'm a hypocrite." That earned him a smile. Truly, though, the sort of help Mary needed was...basic. It was *possible*. She needed an au pair or a good housekeeper, whereas James needed a magical machine to clear away the invisible shrapnel that the war had left inside his skull. He thought he was doing about as well as could be expected in a world where that machine didn't exist. He did his job, even though it wasn't quite the job he had once imagined he'd have. He ate three meals a day, slept most nights. Looking at Marston and the men at the nursing home where he worked at two days a week, he knew how much worse it could be.

"So we agree," Mary said, turning on the tap and rinsing a cup. The dog happily lapped at the stream of water. "We'll just muddle through this world and then hope for better in the next. I've never not muddled, if I'm honest. I'd be quite ill-prepared for a world where things went better than I expected."

"Lucky you, Wendy seems to operate on a plane that's entirely beyond muddling. It's only a matter of time before she stands for parliament or becomes a criminal mastermind, so you ought to give her some honest work to keep her busy. It would do her good," he insisted. "Besides, I'm worried about her since Mrs. Hoggett's death. I think she's taken it hard. Do you know if she has any relations I could contact for her? Did her mother ever leave a forwarding address or get in touch with you in any way?"

The vicar's wife went perfectly still, the only sound the running water. "With me? No, why would she get in touch with me?"

"Weren't you the one who arranged billeting for the children who were evacuated from London," James said, puzzled by the woman's defensiveness.

"There weren't any other children." She took up a dishcloth and swiped it over a bowl that was crusted over with old porridge. "There was only Wendy."

"I see. I was here so infrequently during the war, and I never paid much attention. Isn't that odd, though? Didn't entire schools evacuate to the same village?"

"Perhaps sometimes, when it was done through the authorities. But Wendy was sent here privately."

That surprised James. Wendy had never heard from her mother after she stepped off the train. He wouldn't have thought that a woman who could so blithely abandon her child would have had the forethought or the concern in the first place to arrange for her to leave London for a place of safety.

"Why here?" he asked. "Did Wendy's mother know somebody in the village?"

"I'm afraid I don't remember the details," Mary said with an air of finality, tossing a couple of still-soapy teaspoons onto the draining board.

"I wonder if you still have the paperwork? Whatever forms Wendy's mother filled out? There must have been something."

"It's been over five years, James. Nobody keeps things for that long." She still faced the sink, so James couldn't see her expression, couldn't see whether she was simply tired and annoyed or if she was being deliberately cagey.

"You're saying we don't know who her parents are? There's no birth certificate? Nothing?" He shook his head. "Surely that can't be."

They were interrupted by the vicar's appearance in the kitchen door. "Oh, you're just the man I need, Sommers." The vicar's cheeks were flushed and his voice scratchy. "I have the devil of a sore throat."

James spent the rest of the day diagnosing and treating the tonsillitis cases that had sprung up throughout the village. The matter of Wendy's origins might have sunk in priority, but for the fact that at nearly all the houses he visited, he could hear people whispering about Mildred Hoggett's will.

"I'D REALLY LIKE FOR it to be the gardener," Sally Bright said as she unceremoniously piled the luncheon dishes into the deep kitchen sink. Leo knew the girl was one of Templeton's agents, but in her neat black uniform, she looked very much a proper parlor maid. "He pinches my arse every time he passes me by, and I wouldn't mind watching him swing. Would shoot him myself." She flashed him a vulpine grin. "If that was what king and country wanted from me."

Leo tried to look stern. "I'm going to tell Templeton that spycraft is bad for the morals of today's youth. Stunts their growth and warps their minds." He gazed pointedly at the top of the girl's head, which fell several inches beneath his own.

As far as Leo could tell, there were two types of people in his particular branch of the intelligence services. One sort was a career bureaucrat—Eton, Cambridge, opinions about things like horses and wine. The other type was gleaned from the criminal classes—urchins and runaways with an aptitude for deceit and with nothing and nobody to lose.

Leo was, of course, of the second type. He had gotten picked up by the police after what had to have been his eighth robbery. He had probably been fourteen or fifteen, but had lost track during his time on the street. A man had taken him out of his cell, asked him about his background, quizzed him in the five languages Leo spoke, and the next thing Leo knew he was one of Templeton's agents. That had been fourteen years ago when another war in Europe seemed like something that could be avoided with a bit of deft maneuvering. They had spent a couple of years trying to do just that, buying and selling secrets, intercepting shipments, spying and being spied on. A few well-placed bullets seemed only reasonable, even more so when war finally, inevitably, broke out.

Sally Bright, it seemed, was also of the second type.

"Sod off, you," she said cheerfully. "I don't think it really was the gardener, though, more's the pity. I was the one waiting at the table that night, and I think I would have noticed if he lumbered into the dining room and tampered with anybody's drinks."

"Walk me through that night. Before dinner, when the guests were in the drawing room, who poured the drinks?"

"Colonel Armstrong poured gin and sodas for himself, his secretary, and Mr. and Mrs. Griffiths. The old ladies drank sherry. The doctor only had tea because he knew he might be called away to see to a patient. And the girl—Wendy—had lemonade."

"You were in the drawing room the whole time?"

"I add a decorative air," Sally said, patting her hair.

Leo rolled his eyes, but he knew it was true—a pretty, uniformed maid was as much a status symbol as a new car. Templeton had known what he was about when sending Sally here, even if it seemed a bizarre use of manpower. "Could the colonel have added something to one of the glasses?"

"I don't see why not. But none of them seemed groggy during dinner, which they would have if they had been given a double dose of Veronal before sitting down."

"So, then the phone rang, Dr. Sommers and the housekeeper were called away, and Mrs. Hoggett cleared the glasses and cups from the drawing room while you served dinner."

"Right," Sally confirmed. "You think she took a bit of a tipple from somebody's glass? But the police inspected those glasses and found nothing. Same for the wine glasses at the dinner table."

"It wouldn't take much for a clean glass to be switched out for the one containing Veronal. At dinner, could anyone have reached over and slipped something into another glass?"

"I suppose. So, you think the char was killed by accident, that the Veronal was meant for somebody else, do you? That won't explain how she turned up dead at the bottom of the stairs, though."

"It also doesn't explain why she went upstairs in the first place when she ought to have been in the kitchen."

"She was always sticking her nose where it didn't belong, but haring off upstairs when she ought to have been working was a bit obvious, even for her."

"Tell me where everyone sat at dinner." Leo knew this from the police report, but wanted to hear if retelling the information caused Sally to remember anything.

"The colonel sat at the head of the table, Edith Pickering to his left, then Norris, then the vicar's wife. To the colonel's right were Cora Delacourt, the vicar, Wendy, and an empty seat for the doctor. Nobody sat at the foot of the table."

That meant that if Colonel Armstrong had been the intended victim, only the two old ladies were near enough to have put something into his drink without reaching past another person. "And we're certain Mrs. Clemens didn't add anything to the food before she left."

"Not if she wanted to make sure any certain piece of drugged food land on a particular plate. Besides, you'd taste the Veronal if it were in food. The taste could only be concealed by spirits, wine, coffee. You'd think the wine was corked or the coffee burnt, but you'd probably drink it anyway."

Which was why he kept coming back to the glasses and all but dismissing the faint possibility that the housekeeper might have given the victim a poisoned morsel of food to taste. Leo frowned. "Was there any particular drink that any guest would be certain to drink?" Another thought occurred to him. "Did anybody abstain from wine?"

She pursed her lips thoughtfully. "Wendy, but she's a kid. Edith Pickering had a glass of wine in front of her, but I don't think she drank any. She's the sort who likes to talk about the devil living at the bottom of a bottle. As for the rest of them, I didn't notice, but that doesn't mean anything. I was busy keeping glasses filled and serving dinner—awful work. On my feet 12 hours a day and nary a soul to spare you a kind word. Mrs. Clemens looks at me like I'm about to run off with the silver. Worst assignment I've had, this is."

He raised his eyebrows. "By the looks of you, it's your first assignment."

"No, it ain't."

"You can't be more than seventeen." Not much older than Wendy, who she had dismissed as a mere kid.

Sally put her hands on her hips. "And when did you have your first assignment, mate? You look like one who got into it early."

"Touché." He was impressed that the girl was able to see that much. Maybe she wasn't as green as she looked. Templeton had always been good at picking out canny agents, after all. "Don't you feel that the cap is a trifle much?" he asked, gesturing at the scrap of white lace perched atop her blond head. He couldn't remember the last time he had seen a parlor maid wearing a cap unless it was on stage in a comedy.

"Nah, it was a stroke of genius, this." She fingered the edges of the fabric. "It makes his nibs feel like he's getting something a cut above the ordinary. He pinches every penny, so he went through six housemaids in the year before he hired me. He probably thinks I'm a gift from heaven."

"Hmm," Leo mused. "He's underpaying Norris as well. What's your instinct there?"

She shrugged. "The colonel hollers at him less than he hollers at me, which means he's probably a good secretary. Two reasons I can think of why a person gets underpaid. Either he offers too little because he has ulterior motives"—here she gestured at herself—"or there's something about him that makes people not want to hire him."

"You think he might have a skeleton in his closet? A secret the colonel knew and hired him in spite of?"

"I'd bet a penny to a farthing that Mrs. Hoggett thought so."

"Sally!" called a voice from the stairs. "The colonel will be wanting his tea. Bring an extra cup. He has a guest."

Sally—and it occurred to Leo that Sally was almost certainly not the girl's name—stood up straight and smoothed her apron as the housekeeper approached. "I'll be right upstairs, Mrs. Clemens," she said in an entirely different voice than the bantering tone she had used with Leo. "Mr. Page here was admiring the ruins of the old chapel and came in so he didn't freeze." With that, she disappeared up the stairs with the tea tray.

"Cold weather to be exploring." The housekeeper regarded Leo with narrowed eyes. She was about forty, with sensible shoes, a no-nonsense tweed skirt, and plain blouse. Her dark brown hair was streaked with gray and pulled back severely. Around her neck hung a pair of wire-rimmed spectacles. She had been with Dr. Sommers the night of the murder, so unless she had an accomplice, she was in the clear.

"It was the only leave I could get from work," Leo said with an air of a man thrilled to spend his holiday visiting stately homes and thinking about the masonry techniques of long-dead craftsmen. "We're dreadfully short staffed."

"I see." The suspiciousness of her gaze did not abate by even a fraction, but he couldn't tell if she didn't want him poking around the hall or if she simply distrusted any man who flirted with a teenaged housemaid.

"I heard that the Wych Hall chapel has an especially fine example of—"

"I don't know anything about that," she said, cutting him off. "If you'll excuse me, I have dinner to prepare."

"Oh!" he exclaimed in tones of rapture. "Of course! You're not only Colonel Armstrong's housekeeper, but also the talented cook I keep hearing about. Naturally, I won't keep you from your art." Sometimes he marveled at the tripe he was able to say with a straight face. "But I'd hate to bother the colonel himself about a matter as trifling as stone tracery," Leo said, as if the housekeeper had volunteered Colonel Armstrong's help. "I'm sure he's very busy." He let his voice trail off in a way that begged her to contradict him.

"Well," she said, pursing her lips, "I could see if he might spare a moment."

"Oh, that's so very kind of you!" Leo was all effusiveness. "People in the country are so terribly considerate, aren't they?" Some of the hardness of her features softened—not with warmth so much as exasperation, he guessed—so he pressed on. "So very different from London. Are you any relation of the Northamptonshire Clemenses? I went to school with one of them. Freddie. Died in the war," he added shamelessly. He watched a look of dawning horror spread over the woman's face as she realized she might be forced to listen to a monologue about the fictive Northhamptonshire Clemenses. She was going to deliver him to the colonel and be happy about it.

"Ah, no," she murmured as she led him toward the stairs. "I was born and raised in Wychcomb St. Mary."

Leo made sure they walked slowly up the stairs to the library so he could hear as much as she wanted to say.

JAMES TRUDGED UP TO Wych Hall to check on Colonel Armstrong. The colonel was getting old, and he had trouble with rheumatism and his heart. But when the maid opened the door and showed him into the library, he found the colonel tête-à-tête with Leo Page.

Page was settled into a battered leather armchair, a cigarette in his mouth and a glass of brandy in his hand. There were several cigarette butts in the ashtray beside him. His long legs were crossed at the ankles, and he had the air of a man who was thoroughly enjoying a talk with a like-minded fellow. James was quite confident that nobody had ever enjoyed a conversation with Colonel Armstrong as much as Leo Page was pretending to. It ought to have put him on his guard, the naked deception of the thing. But instead, James found himself charmed. Charmed, of all things, by a spy and a liar, by a man who existed to stir up trouble and—

But, no. Page was just a man. He wasn't the embodiment of the war, and he hadn't come to discompose James's mind. He was only here because something about Mrs. Hoggett's death had caught the attention of somebody at Special Branch. James didn't want to think too hard about what that *something* might be, but whatever it was, it wasn't Page's fault. And right now Page was Wendy's best chance at having a life without a cloud of suspicion following her.

"I think you've met Mr. Page," Colonel Armstrong said to James. "He came to look at the tracery work in the old chapel."

"Have you any triskelions here?" James asked innocently. "We're quite fortunate to have an expert in our midst."

"I've been looking at the pattern of keyhole arches," Page said ingenuously. "Quite unique in this part of England." He spoke with such apologetic avidity that James almost forgot that Page was not, in fact, a devoted enthusiast of stone tracery. "But I've taken up too much of your time already, Colonel Armstrong. Thank you so much for the drink. I wonder if I can borrow your Mr. Norris to show me that bit of the chapel you were mentioning?"

"Yes, of course. Norris!" he bellowed, and the secretary appeared in the doorway of a room that opened off the library. "Norris, show the man that wall, will you."

"The wall, sir?" Norris responded diffidently.

"The east wall, man! The one with the window in it!" He rapped his fist on the arm of his chair as if enraged by the secretary's inability to follow a conversation he had not been present for. James did not care for Norris—there was something squirrely and wrong about him—but he didn't envy the man one jot. The colonel was a beast to work for.

"Ah, quite. I beg your pardon," the secretary answered, totally unruffled. He probably had a good deal of practice being abused by his employer and no longer thought much of it.

Page left with Norris, babbling about high Gothic this and early perpendicular that, his face arranged into an expression of such daft avidity that James had to look away to hide his smile. James spent the next quarter of an hour listening to the colonel's chest and checking his heart, while the colonel complained about the damp, the income tax, and the criminally high price of meat.

"Were you already acquainted with Mr. Page?" James asked while getting ready to leave.

"No, never laid eyes on him before that woman's funeral."

James recalled the colonel's look of shock at the graveside. James had assumed it was seeing Page that had given the colonel such a turn, even though he couldn't figure out why. But if the colonel had been disturbed by seeing Page, he showed no sign of distress now. When James had entered the library, the two men had seemed quite comfortable. But if it hadn't been the sight of Page that had upset Armstrong at the funeral, then what could it have been? He tried to recall where the colonel had been looking the precise moment he had been overcome with surprise. He remembered Mary Griffiths trying to make the twins be quiet, Marston glowering on the edges of the group, Wendy offering him the flask she had found in Mrs. Hoggett's bedroom at Little Briars. But none of that was out of the ordinary.

"Are you headed to Little Briars, Sommers?" Armstrong asked while James shrugged into his coat. He knew perfectly well that James went to check in on the old ladies after visiting Wych Hall, so James only nodded. "Might as well leave through the french doors," the man said with an air of great concession, as he did every week during this moment of magnanimity. "Spare yourself a trip around the house."

The french doors led to a terrace that sloped gently down to the garden. A previous Armstrong—either Armstrong's father or grandfather—had used a wheelchair, and this design of the terrace allowed the man to proceed unaided from the library to the garden. By exiting through the french doors, James could proceed across the terrace to the bottom of the garden and then directly along the footpath through the woods to Little Briars.

"That's very kind of you," James said, as he always did. If the colonel wanted to believe that using the french doors was a special privilege, James could indulge him.

James wasn't surprised to find Page waiting for him at the edge of the woods, hidden by shadow.

"You're going to get a chest cold," James said by way of greeting, despite knowing perfectly well the weather had nothing to do with the spread of disease. "You aren't even wearing a muffler," he added reproachfully. Page had the collar of his coat turned up against the wind, but despite years of medical training, James couldn't rid himself of the superstition that an exposed neck might worsen tonsillitis. "Did Norris tell you what you wanted to know?" James asked.

"Now, what makes you think I had an ulterior motive in wanting to spend time with a man who looks like that?"

"Please," James scoffed.

Page laughed softly. "No, my taste runs more to handsome doctors who worry about people catching cold. And he didn't tell me a damn thing. He was as nervous as a hare. Are we walking back through the village or taking the footpath through the wood?"

James noticed the easy assumption that they'd walk together, and was aware that he liked it a bit too much. "The footpath," he said, leading the way. "I want to stop in at Little Briars."

"Is today your day for checking on the elderly?"

"It's my day for taking walks in the woods with dangerous strangers," James said, surprised to find he still had the knack for light flirtation.

"Ha. Will the ladies invite me in for tea?"

"Good God," James said. "You'll be lucky if you get away that easily. They'll insist on stuffing you with biscuits and regaling you with tales of Cora's misspent youth."

"I think I'd rather like that," Page said. "It's been a long time since my work involved grannies and biscuits." Was that a note of wistfulness in his voice? A gust of wind whipped through the woods, rustling bare branches and causing Page to draw his coat more tightly around himself.

"Here, take my muffler." James began unwinding it from his neck.

"I can't—"

"I have three just like it. Edith is forever knitting the things. She started making them for soldiers during the war and never got out of the habit." James stopped walking and looped the scarf around Page's neck. Page must have recognized this as the obvious approach that it was because his mouth quirked up in a half smile as he took a step to close the gap between them. The fronts of their coats were brushing against one another, and James could feel the heat of the other man's breath on his cheek.

"I'm not wearing your scarf," Page said, unwrapping it from his neck and replacing it around James's but not letting go of the ends. "It won't do for anyone to notice that I'm wearing your clothes. Even discreet outer layers."

"Ah. These are the delicate workings of an intelligence officer's mind, I see."

Page kept hold of the scarf but stepped even closer to James, thereby maneuvering him back against a tree. James let himself be moved. He could feel the cold and roughness of the bark through his coat, while in front of him he was caged in by the hard heat of Page.

James's heart pounded in his chest. He tried to tell himself that it was because it had been a matter of years since he had so much as kissed a man, since he had touched anyone for any purpose other than tending to their ailments and injuries. But the fact was that James hadn't wanted to touch anyone since the war. This kindling interest he had in Page was something of a relief, proof that the war hadn't taken that from him along with so much else. In every other respect, this attraction was disconcerting: Page was dangerous. James' sanity depended on believing that the village was a safe and orderly place, and Page's presence exposed that as a fairy story.

Maybe Page saw some of that conflict on his face because instead of leaning in to kiss him, he stood perfectly still with a quizzical expression that James couldn't quite interpret. Then he leaned back fractionally and produced a cigarette seemingly out of thin air. "You're right," Page said, lighting the cigarette. "It's cold. Let's go drink some tea and be civil."

Chapter 6

"Christ," Page said as they approached Little Briars. The sun was setting, but there was enough light to make out the building's unusual silhouette. James had known this place his entire life, but now he tried to imagine seeing it through Page's eyes. It had initially been a farmhouse, probably dating from the sixteenth century. But it had been added to in a higgledy-piggledy manner over the years, and now boasted an agglomeration of gables and wings in various architectural styles. Chimney pots poked out in unlikely places and the scattershot arrangement of windows hinted that the interior of the house might reflect the outside.

"It looks like a gingerbread house assembled by a thoroughly mad child," Page said. He took a puff from his cigarette and stepped a few paces to the side as if to survey the house from a different angle. "I love it."

James felt absurdly relieved. It wouldn't have mattered if Page thought Little Briars a chaotic mess. It was only a house, not even his own house, and besides, it wasn't like a man's opinion on architecture cancelled out his being a...whatever it was Page was.

"I'll bring you around to the front," James said. They had approached the house from the back, through the woods.

"What's that over there?" Page gestured towards a small structure in the corner of the garden.

"That's Wendy's hen house." The girl had built it with her own two hands that spring, using boards she had pried loose from a derelict shed and a box of nails she found in the cellar.

"I meant the garden." He let out a low whistle. "This is more a small farm than a kitchen garden."

"That's also Wendy's doing. She started it as a victory garden and it got rather out of hand."

"This must produce more than she and the two old ladies can eat."

"Indeed it does. She kept the village in vegetable marrows and potatoes all autumn, to say nothing of the eggs. By the way, I asked Mrs. Griffiths about Wendy's family, and apparently, she was brought to Little Briars by some kind of private arrangement." James didn't like repeating this information to an outsider, knowing that Page would interpret it as proof something was amiss with the girl. "And she's mislaid the paperwork." When the silence between them dragged on, he felt compelled to add, "I'm afraid she's rather scatterbrained. I'm sure there's a perfectly reasonable explanation."

"Are you, though?" Page asked.

"Yes," James insisted.

Leo regarded him levelly for a moment before giving him a slight smile that seemed tinged with pity.

AS SOMMERS HAD FORETOLD, the ladies of Little Briars welcomed Leo and gave him tea, biscuits, and anecdotes. Within half a minute of walking through the door, he was drinking criminally sweet tea and poring over a book of photographs featuring a very young and pretty Miss Delacourt in full Edwardian regalia. He now sat on a chair near the fire, drowsy from the heat and the surfeit of sweets. On the sofa opposite him, Sommers shrugged out of his jacket and draped it over the arm of his chair, and Leo gratefully followed suit.

Cora Delacourt had to be 70. In the photo album that rested on Leo's lap, there were blurry photographs of Miss Delacourt with a portly Prince of Wales—Miss Delacourt must have been quite fast indeed—taken a good fifty years earlier. In the fluffy, bespectacled, white-haired lady who repeatedly offered him biscuits, Leo could see traces of the Edwardian belle in the photographs before him. In several of the pictures, a thin and grim-faced woman looked on; this Leo recognized immediately as Miss Pickering. Edith Pickering had the sort of austere features and fine bones that changed little with age. He realized that this book of photographs was the documentation of a life spent together, half a century lived side by side, one woman a blur of ribbons and flounces on a passing bicycle, the other a constant, watchful presence.

Leo was used to not having a family; he was used to not having a place where he belonged or people he belonged to. But looking at these women and knowing they had spent a lifetime together made him think it was a failure on his part that he hadn't managed to even acquire friends.

He hoped with all his heart that his next case would bring him to a proper den of thieves, someplace lousy with crime and crawling with unprincipled mercenaries and he could be reminded of what sensible priorities looked like. He wasn't cut out for old ladies and tea.

"Have another scone," Miss Delacourt said brightly, jolting him back to the present. "And try some of this marmalade. Wendy made it."

Leo took a bite of the scone, letting the sharp tang of citrus distract him from his train of thought.

"Dare I ask where Wendy got the sugar?" Sommers eyed his half-eaten scone with a sort of guilty hunger. "Last I heard, she used all her coupons on peppermint creams for the children at the vicarage."

"She's very resourceful," Miss Delacourt said dubiously, and Leo inferred this meant the girl was up to shenanigans that were not entirely above board.

Leo turned the page and saw a photograph of an elderly man in a clerical collar and a serious-faced boy in short pants. With a start, Leo realized the boy was Dr. Sommers. He glanced up and saw the same grave expression, the same cowlick disordering his hair, the same smattering of freckles. He flipped the page again, and there was Sommers as a young man, before the war, his handsome face lit by a smile. He didn't quite know why it bothered him to see this proof that Sommers belonged here, in this place, with these people, but he decided it was an excellent time to do some reconnaissance. He excused himself to go to the washroom.

Upstairs there was a corridor with six doors. Two he identified as an airing cupboard and the washroom, which meant the remaining four were likely bedrooms. Behind the first of these doors, he found a room littered with odd numbers of socks and featuring an unmade bed. He didn't risk flicking the light switch, but his pocket torch showed him the muddy shoes Wendy had been wearing at the funeral. He stepped back into the corridor and opened the next door. A narrow bed, a dresser empty except for a fine layer of dust—about a week's worth, which meant they hadn't hired a new cleaning lady since Mrs. Hoggett's death, and also that nobody regularly used this room. The third room contained a large bed, with a drinking glass on one bedside table and a bible on the other. Miss Delacourt's, perhaps? He opened the fourth and final door, expecting to see a similar bedroom belonging to the other old lady, but instead found a very small room with its contents half packed into boxes, meaning it had to be the dead charwoman's quarters. Which meant he was short a bedroom, unless—oh. *Oh.* The two night tables in one room, the dust in the other. So, the two elderly women shared a bedroom. They were a couple. He ought to have gathered as much from the fifty years of photographs. That rather warmed his bombed out shell of a heart.

Still, even if they were as queer as he was, it didn't mean they weren't murderers. Mrs. Hoggett could perhaps have noticed their secret and attempted to blackmail them. The incongruity of that thought—those two old ladies as murderers—jolted him to awareness. He really wasn't cut out for tea and gossip if he started seeing skeletons in the closets of elderly women.

Treading lightly so the floorboards wouldn't creak and give away his explorations, he returned to the end of the hall to the tiny room that had been Mrs. Hoggett's. His torch held under one arm and a pair of leather gloves on his hands, he deftly searched every drawer, every inch of the place. It was good, he thought, to remind himself why he was really here. He was here to violate the space of a dead woman, not to befriend old ladies, not to kiss handsome doctors in the wood. This was just what he needed to put himself back in his place.

JAMES REALIZED HIS error even before Page sat on the overstuffed armchair.

The sight of Page in Cora and Edith's drawing room, Edith's pretty rose-patterned teacup in his hands and Cora's book of photographs open on his lap, stripped the man of all his dangerous associations and turned him into a person—a warm, living, laughing person. A person who made conversation with the people James loved, a person who drank tea and let old ladies give him too many biscuits. It was so ordinary, so commonplace, so utterly disarming.

James sank back into the sofa cushions and allowed his gaze to travel over Page's lean form, let himself appreciate how good the other man looked in his shirtsleeves, cuffs rolled back to reveal lean forearms dusted with dark hair. It was a lapse in judgment, letting himself be drawn to a man like this. But even after Page excused himself—presumably to look for clues in Edith's knitting basket or engage in some other act of subterfuge—he couldn't quite muster up the outrage he knew he would have felt a few days earlier. Because now Page wasn't just a spy: he was a person who—like James himself—had been in the war and now took comfort in an overheated parlor and a well-worn photo album. James at least could have this whenever he wished; God only knew what Page's future held.

His thoughts were interrupted by squawking from the garden, followed by the sound of a door being thrown open and booted feet stomping through the kitchen.

"I don't know what you've been feeding those hens, Wendy," Edith called, "but if they're going to fuss like that every time you walk past, we'll have to move the coop away from the house." The woman's tone was brisk, but a note of indulgence underlay her words. "I realize the world is upside down, but we must cling to some niceties."

"I ought to stop feeding them altogether and stew them up," Wendy said, flinging herself onto the sofa beside James. She wore a pair of disreputable looking boots and an old men's overcoat that dwarfed her, and the cold wafted off the wool of her clothes. "They're so lazy in this weather that I haven't gotten so much as a single egg all week."

"It's just as well," James said, placing a cup of tea on the table before the girl. "Eggs would freeze in this cold. Mrs. Murphy's pipes burst yesterday while I was seeing to Freddie's tonsils."

"I saw Freddie at the pond and he said he'll have to have them out."

James suppressed a slight shudder at the thought of blood and scalpels, the smell of the operating theater.

"It would be better if it snowed," Cora murmured, then narrowed her eyes as she took in Wendy's ensemble. "Tell me you haven't been wearing that all day, Wendy dear. We have company—the gentleman from London who was at the funeral. He'll be back downstairs any minute now and he won't know what to think if he sees you dressed like a scarecrow."

"Isn't it funny," Wendy said as she pulled off her gloves, "that we went months and months without seeing a new face, and then all of a sudden we have a new housemaid at Wych Hall, that cousin who visited you, and now Mr. Page?" She cupped her hands around her mouth to warm them with her breath.

"What cousin?" James asked, picking up the girl's gloves from her lap and folding them neatly.

"Nobody interesting," Wendy said mournfully, reminding James of Polly Griffiths complaining about beef tea. "Some old man visited Miss Delacourt. Mr. Tarmington? No, he had a title. Balding and tweedy. You know, James, I don't think they were cousins at all. I think he was one of her beaux."

"Wendy!" Edith reproached, but Cora only laughed.

"I'm afraid she's onto me," Cora said. "Although, how lowering it is that in all these years, only one beau has cared enough to visit me in my waning years."

"The rest are probably dead," Wendy said comfortingly. The two women stared at her for a moment, eyes wide.

"Wendy!" James said. "You can't say that sort of thing."

But then Edith and Cora started to laugh. James didn't think he had ever heard Edith laugh. She looked like she might keel right over. "It's all right, James," Edith said once she had gotten control of herself. "We know we're old. Oh, Wendy, I meant to tell you. There are three very drunk mice in the pantry."

"Mice? Oh! The Christmas pudding!" Wendy shot to her feet. "I mustn't have covered it properly. Oh, bother. Nobody will want pudding mice have gotten to."

"More urgently," Edith said, "something needs to be done about the mice. I can't stoop to pick up mice or anything else."

"Feed them to the cat," Cora suggested mildly. "Perhaps if she has a full belly she'll keep away from Wendy's chickens."

James tried to drag his mind away from the gruesome image of greedy snapping kitchen cats gobbling up half-dead mice, but his stomach turned anyway. This was a new and irritating development. He had thought he could count on his mind behaving itself in Edith and Cora's sitting room, surrounded by butter biscuits and milky tea. Was he to spend the rest of his days shaken by any mention of unpleasantness? Were bombs and blood to follow him into every safe haven he created for himself?

"I'll put them outside. It's my fault," Wendy said, moving toward the door. When James looked up at her, he saw Page standing in the doorway. He didn't know how long the man had been there.

"I don't know what we're going to do about that girl," Edith said after they heard the back door shut and the chickens send up their equivalent of a cheer. "She's fifteen. Shouldn't be mucking about with chickens and traipsing about the village dressed like a farmhand." She pulled a wad of knitting out of her work basket and began stitching as if the wool had done her a gross injustice and being made up into a muffler was a proper revenge. "She ought to be going to dances and trimming bonnets or whatever it is girls do these days."

"Doesn't she go to school?" Page asked.

"She finished early," Edith said. "Either she's quite clever or the headmistress was happy to see the back of her. Probably both."

"Well, dear, when I think of what you and I were up to at that age, I daresay we would have been safer at home with the chickens," Cora said placidly, topping Page's cup off with tepid tea and catching Edith's eye.

When they stepped outside, the cold air was almost a relief. James hadn't lost the queasy feeling, the sense of imminent doom. He needed to go home, sit in the dark, and probably take one of the pills that he saved for emergencies. And wasn't that a pitiful thought—that a stray mention of dead mice and a minor surgery counted as an emergency. James didn't know what would become of him in the event he was confronted with something truly disturbing.

"Are you going to be all right?" Page asked after they had walked in silence down the drive from Little Briars.

"Quite," James snapped. He supposed his mental state was common knowledge now. First Mary Griffiths, now Page. Apparently one could tell just from looking at him that he wasn't quite right in the head. Not, he reflected grimly, an ideal quality in a doctor.

"Naturally," Page said easily, after only the barest hesitation.

At the place where the lane forked, in one direction heading through the wood to Wych Hall and the other to the village, Page announced that he needed to go back to Wych Hall, presumably to spy on its inhabitants. James reminded himself that this was why he needed to stay away from the man, needed to keep clear of things that would put him in a place where he couldn't even trust his own mind. But through all his muddled thoughts, past the racing of his heart, he mainly worried that Page would catch cold.

"Take the damned muffler, Page," he insisted, shoving it at the man with none of their earlier intimacy. "Otherwise, you'll be the only one within twenty furlongs of Little Briars without one."

Page shook his head and stepped backward, vanishing into the shadows.

LEO TOOK THE FOOTPATH through the woods, passing the cottage where the shell-shocked beekeeper lived. It was only six, but long since dark, and only a single light burned inside the cottage's small windows. He kept walking until he reached the garden gate that gave access to Wych Hall. From there, he could see the terrace that skirted the back of the house and the french doors of Colonel Armstrong's library. Little Briars had been empty the night of the murder; a person could have come from the village, through the woods, through the french doors, with only the chance of being witnessed by one person who didn't seem to have much interest in the outside world.

It shouldn't have come as a relief to discover that a stranger might have committed the murder. In fact, it was utter nonsense, and Leo knew it. It was entirely implausible to think that a stranger had slipped into the house, somehow poisoned a charwoman, and then pushed her down the stairs. The fact that it had occurred to Leo at all was a sign that he wasn't thinking straight about this case.

The sound of a throat clearing made him reach for the pistol he kept in the holster under his coat.

"Mr. Page," Mr. Norris said. "What a pleasure to see you twice in one day."

"I left my cigarette lighter," Page said, transforming his grab for the pistol into a sheepish shrug. And, in fact, he had left the lighter in the kitchen to provide an excuse for his return. "Are you taking a walk? It's a bit cold, I would have thought."

"Come over here and I'll show you what I'm doing," Norris said.

Page hoped the man didn't intend to murder him. He was not in the mood for disposing of a corpse this evening. One hand casually on the hilt of a knife he kept sheathed in his coat pocket, he followed the secretary.

They didn't have long to wait. As they stood in the shadows of the ruined Wych Hall chapel, Leo saw a figure emerge from the wood and poke through the shrubbery. The figure had a pair of untidy black plaits peeking out from beneath a knit cap.

"This is three nights running that Wendy Smythe has been prowling about," Norris said. "If I didn't know better I'd think she was looking for something. Perhaps she lost her lighter too."

With that, Norris bade Leo good night and returned to the house.

Chapter 7

Tonsillitis kept James blessedly busy during the next day, and it was nearly midnight when he staggered up the walk to his house. As he approached his front door, a lean silhouette emerged from the shadows.

"It's only me." It was Leo Page. As if there were anyone else who would be lurking on his doorstep.

"What the hell are you doing skulking about like that?" James demanded.

"I wasn't skulking." He took a step nearer so James could see his face clearly. Page's dark hair shone almost black in the moonlight. "I was waiting for you. That's entirely different."

"Why the devil didn't you send a note? People don't stand about in weather like this. You'll scare somebody to death. And it's not healthy. You're not even wearing a hat," he added, realizing he sounded like an old lady. Even in the dark, he thought he could see Page's mouth curling upwards.

"Maybe you'll invite me in, then," he said softly. "For my health."

James drew in a sharp breath. There was no mistaking Page's meaning. James knew it was wiser to decline, safer to proceed alone as usual into his empty house. But he saw Page's breath clouding faintly in the darkness and wanted to be closer. He had meant to barricade himself safely in the confines of routine and order until his mind settled down. At the moment, though, there was no end in sight—it could mean a lifetime without sex, without companionship, without even close friendship. But he didn't want to be alone indefinitely. It didn't seem fair. And wasn't that laughable—demanding that war wounds do the decent thing and not trouble one overmuch.

Stepping past Page, he fumbled in his pocket for his latchkey. He felt Page's eyes on him as he turned the key in the lock and crossed into the darkened foyer. He flicked on the lamp near the door and got a good look at Page's face, which was white with cold.

"I'll start a fire," he said, taking off his topcoat, "after I put the kettle on."

Page turned in the hall, not making any effort to conceal that he was taking stock of his surroundings. James wondered what it looked like through his eyes. The surgery took up half the ground floor, but still, the house was too big for a bachelor; without patients its silence was conspicuous, the air stale and cold. He had bought the house from the old doctor at the same time he bought the practice, acquiring house, furniture, patient list, and receptionist all at once. When he had come back from France, he could think of nothing he wanted more than to return to Wychcomb St. Mary. The doctor's retirement seemed nothing less than providential. James had stepped wholesale into the role of country doctor with the relief of stepping into a warm towel after a cold bath, but imagining it through Page's eyes made him feel like a child who had been caught trying on his father's shoes.

"I would have thought you'd have a housekeeper and a hot dinner waiting for you," Page remarked, hanging his hat and coat on pegs behind the door.

"A village woman comes in every morning to clean out the surgery and twice a week to make a couple of suppers and tidy up downstairs a bit." James peeled off his own coat and hung it beside Page's, then put his black bag on the floor beneath. The bag, too, had been the old doctor's. He stepped into the kitchen, then lit the stove and put the kettle on the hob. "But tonight it's tinned soup and cold sandwiches."

Page shot him a frankly flirtatious glance. "Are you inviting me to stay for supper?"

James hadn't thought that far. He glanced at the can of soup that sat beside the hob. He had meant to warm it up and eat it alone at the kitchen table while solving that day's crossword and listening to the wireless. That was how he spent his evenings when he wasn't invited out to dinner or called away to a patient. He was dimly aware that he wanted Page to be several hundred miles away—Moscow or Bolivia or wherever people like him plied their trade—but also simultaneously in his bed. The middle ground of sharing a meal with him alone in an empty house seemed dangerously intimate.

"I'm not sure whether I'm inviting you for supper or trying to treat a hypothermia case," he said, striving for lightness. "Here, I'll go lay the fire and you pour the water when it boils. Tea is in the cupboard, cups are in the board by the sink. Can you manage or are your hands numb?"

Page's expression was amused. "You do realize I'm no stranger to uncomfortable conditions, don't you? I didn't spend my youth snug by the fire."

James was struck anew by the fact that he had a spy in his kitchen. He half expected his windows to shatter with an exploding shell, the air to fill with the smell of smoke and death.

He ran his hands over the rough surface of the old refectory table, keeping his gaze locked on the faded wallpaper with its cheerful roosters presiding over baskets of improbably grouped flowers and fruits.

"Neither did you," Page added. "We both were very busy for a few years there, I daresay, but the war is over now," he said softly, and James looked over, startled, unsure how Page had known precisely what was in his mind. He supposed spies made it their business to read minds. "You're safe," Page went on.

"It's not about that," James said, knowing he sounded petulant. "I'm not worried about my own safety." And, rationally, he wasn't. It would just be extremely convenient if his entire brain could get on board with that knowledge. He swallowed. "I was going to get filthy drunk tonight."

"Don't let me stop you. But what were you going to be, ah, drinking about?"

James debated a convenient falsehood, but more deception was the last thing he needed in his dealings with Leo Page. "I don't like you being here."

A shadow passed across Page's face. "You aren't meant to. It's an ugly business. Sometimes I don't like it much myself. But it's necessary. Like cleaning out the chimney."

"I don't mean the..." he gestured vaguely. "Spycraft, or what have you. What I don't like is what it means. It's as if the war didn't end and never will end. How do we go on knowing that people are willing to blow one another up, again and again? Cut one another to bits. Twice in half a century, Page. Are we going to keep doing this?"

"No," Page said swiftly, as if he had already thought about this. "Now there are atom bombs. That changes things."

James thought he was going to be sick. "That's not comforting."

"It's not meant to be. Listen, Sommers. War isn't the worst thing people are capable of. The people I killed in the war—most of them at least—were Nazis. The men you patched up, you did it so they could go out and kill more Nazis. Some things are worth blood and guts."

"I know that," James protested. "But..." How could he explain that sometimes when he shut his eyes, he saw nothing but death, nothing but the piles of gore and flesh that people turned one another into? "My head is a mess."

Page stepped closer. "That's all of us, mate."

"No, I assure you that I'm farther gone than most. And I wasn't even a soldier. All I did was, as you said, stitch people up. What right do I have to—"

"No." Page laid a hand on his shoulder. "What you're not going to do is talk about shell shock or combat fatigue or brain fuckery as if it's a special treat that you haven't earned."

James huffed out a startled laugh. "I know that. Thank you. I—"

"Shut up." Page was very close now, his hand still heavy on James's shoulder. He smelled of cigarette smoke and hair pomade, second-hand shops and shaving soap. All James needed to do was lean in, angle his head, and they would be kissing. That would earn him some time, a reprieve from the ghosts that lived in his head, the sort of distraction he hadn't had in too long. But he felt the cold radiating off the man. First things first.

James went into the parlor to light the fire. He usually relied on the heat from the stove, and then a hot water bottle in his bed, but it was bitterly cold, and Page looked like he needed something more. With shaky hands, James set about lighting the kindling. Damn it. It was only a fire. And he was only lighting it for the comfort of a man who looked like he could use some. After a few minutes of rearranging twigs and fanning flames, he had the fire going. He sat back on his heels to admire his work.

Some minutes later, Page appeared in the doorway carrying two cups of tea. He had taken off his coat. "That's a proper fire. Where did you get firewood?" asked Page from the doorway.

"It's from Marston." James had been saving it, but he wasn't going to tell Page so.

"Is that allowed?"

"A tree fell on Marston's land, and he gave me some of the firewood when I splinted his broken finger. But if you'd like to report me for black market procurement of firewood, please, by all means, go ahead."

Page snorted. "I'll resist the urge."

James took the proffered cup of tea and watched as Page sat beside him on the hearthrug, cross-legged. "How did you know how I take my tea?" he asked after taking a sip. It was black and not very sweet.

"I noticed at the vicarage and then again at Little Briars."

James supposed Page was in the business of noticing things. He frowned. "What did you come here to tell me? What was so urgent that you had to freeze at my door?" He saw in the set of the other man's jaw what he ought to have known as soon as he saw the man in the dark: he hadn't come for flirtation. He was here for work. He had learned something.

Page looked at him over the rim of his cup, his eyes flashing darkly. "I don't know if I want to spoil things by telling you."

"There's nothing to spoil," James lied.

"I'm cold, and I'm tired, and I'd like to pretend that we're just two men in an empty house, enjoying one other's company." Page sipped his tea but didn't take his eyes off James. "Whatever that means is up to you."

There was no room for doubt in Page's words. James swallowed. "I've never been good at pretending."

"Ah, but I'm good enough for both of us." He didn't move any closer to James. He was dropping that decision in James's lap.

James kept his gaze on the fire, focused on the smell and warmth of the wood fire, the worn carpet beneath him. He was in Wychcomb St. Mary, he was safe, there was peace—and there was no such thing as safety or peace. Maybe it was simply that it had been so long since James made a bad decision that he had forgotten what it felt like, or maybe he just wanted to be reminded that bodies could be warm and well and alive. He turned to face Page and cupped his jaw in one hand. Page went still, then raised an eyebrow.

"Doctor," Page began.

"Oh, be quiet," James said, and closed the gap. He took Page's face in between his still-cold hands and stroked his thumbs over the man's cheekbones. Too tenderly for a man this dangerous, too slow for people with no future. Any more time with Page would cut him open and expose all his weaknesses, but for a moment before the hearth, he let himself imagine it was possible. He allowed himself to enjoy the illusion for a moment, then turned his head away.

"Tell me why you came here tonight," James said, his heart still pounding, his body asking for more.

Page sighed, and James didn't miss the disappointment that flickered across the other man's face. "I feel this is a conversation best had at a polite distance," Page said, gracefully getting to his feet and regarding the fire. The flickering light transformed him into a dark, dangerous silhouette. Was it James's imagination or was Page's accent different than it had been a few moments ago? James had thought the man had a west country accent, but now his voice had a refined polish. He scrambled onto his own feet with much less grace than Page had managed.

"So?" James asked.

"Well, then. I saw Wendy at Wych Hall last night, searching through the bushes. Norris saw her too. She had a torch. I think you need to prepare yourself for the possibility that Wendy Smythe has something to hide, and that it's not going to stay hidden for long."

LEO KNEW WHAT IT LOOKED like when a man was being confronted with a set of facts that made him rethink everything he thought he knew, and now he was watching it happen to Dr. Sommers.

"Surely she might have had a reason to be there?" the doctor protested, his arms folded across his chest. "She traipses all over the countryside, sometimes on foot, sometimes on that rickety old pushbike. She had just been there earlier that day. Maybe she dropped something."

"Could be," Leo said dubiously.

"You can't—are you saying that you think she was return-ing to the scene of the crime?" Sommers shook his head, plainly dumbfounded. Another man might have been angry, but Som-mers looked confused and disappointed—disappointed, Leo realized, in Leo for harboring suspicions of Wendy Smythe.

Leo took out a cigarette, more because he wanted to look at something other than Sommers coming to grips with the fact that he, Leo, was an evil-minded bastard and this girl Wendy might be even worse. "She was near the french doors leading to Armstrong's library."

"You can't think—"

"I'm not sure I do. After all, if Wendy wanted to kill this woman, she could have done it in any number of ways more convenient than waiting for the middle of a dinner party. Their bedrooms were four paces apart from one another." If Sommers realized this meant Leo had snooped upstairs at Little Briars, he didn't betray any surprise. "I need your help in finding out what she was doing there. And, Dr. Sommers?"

"Yes?"

"It's in my interest that Mildred Hoggett's death not be the subject of an official investigation. But if Wendy is poking around at the scene of the crime, other people will notice. And then the local authorities will have no choice but to act. I would dearly like to prevent that from happening." Without paying much attention, he had put on the accent he used to impress people like Colonel Armstrong, as somebody might put on their best coat, and now he felt gauchely overdressed.

The doctor's face clouded. Probably he had the honest man's instinctive distaste for subverting the course of justice.

That was a luxury Leo never had. If only honest men knew how many lives had been saved with a bit of criminal conspiracy, they'd think it one of the cardinal virtues. This was probably how butchers felt when someone felt sorry for pigs while halfway through a ham sandwich.

Speaking of which. "I'll leave you to your supper, Dr. Sommers." He could have charmed his way back into the doctor's good graces. He probably could have gotten the man into bed if he wanted to. But he didn't need Sommers to like him. He had always been able to take or leave the sort of thing the doctor was offering—a bit of pleasure, that was all. Anything else was for other men. Leo had forgotten that, and Sommers' reaction was a timely reminder.

For a moment he thought Sommers would renew his invitation to stay for supper. But then he shook his head as if to dislodge the idea that Leo was somebody he wanted to spend time with. "Good night, Mr. Page. Try to stay warm. Maybe whatever it is you need to do could wait for some sunshine."

They both knew this was nonsense. Leo would be spending the next few hours with no company but an electric torch, combing the bushes at Wych Hall for whatever it was Wendy Smythe had been looking for. That wasn't something that could be done in the daytime. Maybe some of that was visible on his face, or maybe Sommers realized that on his own, because before Leo could say anything, Sommers took his muffler from a peg by the door and looped it around Leo's neck. The scratch of the wool sent electricity coursing through his nerve endings as much as any caress might.

"At least try not to freeze to death," Sommers said. "Even if you are used to it."

And so Leo went into the night, wrapped in a wool muffler that smelled of antiseptic soap and slow caresses by a rare wood fire, a reminder of an honest man who still wanted to keep him warm.

Chapter 8

The next morning the Griffiths children still had a fever, which was only to be expected. But they seemed properly put out by being confined to bed, which was an excellent sign. James prescribed further rest. Slightly more concerning was the vicar's condition.

"He's still in bed," Mary Griffiths said as she led James to the bedroom. "And he has on his silk pajamas. They haven't made an appearance since he had his appendix out last year."

After taking the vicar's temperature and examining his throat, James frowned. "I'm afraid you're going to need something more than rest and beef tea."

Griffiths groaned. He was shivering with the fever and his eyes were glassy. "Go away, Sommers," he rasped.

"No such luck, old boy. You need something to kill the bacteria that are wreaking havoc on your body. You've a fever of a hundred and four."

"I don't want your snake oil. Made me sick as a dog last time I had that stuff."

That stuff was Prontosil, an antibacterial drug used to treat infections. "Last time you were sick as a dog before you even took the medicine."

"It gave me a rash."

It never ceased to amaze James how ordinarily rational, clear-thinking men could become superstitious and addle-brained when it came to medicine. The vicar had waited to have his appendix removed until the thing was ready to burst, and even then it had taken some doing for Mary to get him to the hospital.

"It might have done," James said, closing his bag, "or it may have been the illness itself that caused the rash. In any event, a rash is better than letting your brain roast inside your skull from fever. I'll call the chemist and have them send a bottle over." The children upstairs would do fine without the drugs. But Griffiths was fifty years old and not in the best of health.

Griffiths grumbled unintelligibly. "If you're calling the chemist, have them put together a jar of Mary's nerve tonic. Her bottle went missing."

"Nerve tonic?" James repeated. "I've never prescribed Mary anything of the sort."

"Wasn't you. She's had it for years," the vicar rasped. "She never takes it, but carries it about in her bag like a lucky rabbit's foot. But the other day she dumped out her bag when she was looking for her spare keys and realized she couldn't remember the last time she had seen the Veronal."

James nearly asked whether they had thought to mention the missing barbiturates to the police, but then thought better of it. The thought of somebody rifling through Mary's bag, stealing medicine, and using it to murder Mrs. Hoggett brought home the reality that if Mrs. Hoggett had been murdered, it had been by someone they all knew. "I'll speak with her," James managed. "Meanwhile, take the medicine when the chemist delivers it."

"I'm telling you," Mary said when James left the vicar's room. "He's harder to nurse than the children. I'm half run off my feet with the lot of them."

"Are you feeling poorly?" James eyed her carefully. She didn't look feverish, but it would be a surprise if she didn't catch what the rest of her family had.

"I don't have time to feel poorly," she grumbled.

"Do ask Wendy," James suggested once again. Wendy always seemed happy to function as childminder and general dogsbody at the vicarage. "She loves you and your children."

For some reason, this made Mary shift and look away. "I feel badly asking her, if I'm being honest. She does so much here already. All the ivy and holly that's hanging about the parlor is her doing. And only last week she built a cucumber frame in the kitchen garden."

"I didn't know you had a kitchen garden," James said.

"We don't. Rather, we did a few years ago, but it died because I didn't know what I was doing and Daniel's no help. But Wendy says we have a patch of ground with good soil and there's no reason we shouldn't grow vegetable marrows the size of our heads and eat like kings. I can't say I'd want a vegetable marrow the size of my head, but she seemed intent. At any rate, she built the frame and promised to till the soil and plant seeds in the spring."

"And so she will. You've seen what she did with the garden at Little Briars. They were drowning in courgettes this summer. Speaking of Wendy, would you mind looking through Daniel's papers and see if you can find anything about Wendy's parents? I know you said they were missing, but I can't imagine Daniel throwing out important paperwork. I hate to pester you, but it's for legal reasons. Something to do with a trust," he lied, the falsehood sour on his tongue.

"Oh." She sounded surprised and dismayed. "I'll look, but don't get your hopes up."

James had always thought the vicar was the kind of scatterbrained person who saved every scrap of paper, not the type to throw them out. He frowned. "There has to be something showing who she is."

She sighed. "The children were babies and I was out of my head, if you recall."

James hadn't been living here at the time and he didn't remember any of this. "Was that when the old doctor prescribed you Veronal?"

Mary looked up sharply. "Daniel told you about that, did he?"

"I don't suppose you have any ideas of who might have taken it from your handbag?"

She let out a mirthless laugh. "We both know I leave the thing around the village more days than I remember to keep it by me."

He left the vicarage in a much grimmer mood than he had entered it. Mary wasn't being entirely forthright at the moment, not about the Veronal nor about Wendy's paperwork. Perhaps she was embarrassed about having lost both the drugs and Wendy's paperwork. Perhaps she had misgivings about having placed Wendy without the proper documentation. He knew, logically, that there were all kinds of reasons for people to have secrets, most perfectly innocent. In all likelihood, Wendy's mother had been a disreputable friend of somebody in the village, and everybody thought her better forgotten, for Wendy's sake.

But what if Mrs. Hoggett had found out? Was it possible that she, while cleaning at the vicarage, had put her nose where it didn't belong and found something about Wendy's mother? Would any secret about Wendy's origin be enough to incite murder?

Between this and the missing Veronal, James couldn't escape the knowledge that there might be a killer nearby, walking among them in the village, as it were. It would be a daily reminder of death, of the fact that people sometimes killed one another on a grand scale, with flags waving and songs in their heart, with the roar of guns and the smell of rot. He had thought that at Wychcomb St. Mary he'd be safe from those memories.

Scarcely paying attention to where he was going, he made his way from the vicarage to the train station—it was one of his days at the convalescent home, and he was already late—but found himself standing before the church. It was a path he had taken hundreds upon hundreds of times as a boy, running errands for his uncle. He sat in the rearmost pew and let his gaze drift to the window of the three hares. His uncle had argued that it was a symbol of the holy trinity, but also a representation of past, present, and future, all tangled together, infinitely cyclical, and in the end, indistinguishable from one another. As a child, he had found this comforting. No matter what—dead fathers, mothers who abandoned one without so much as a goodbye—the future was always in wait with its promise of hope and renewal. Now he found himself thinking of how if the three hares represented past, present, and future, that meant the future was always touched by the past. Chased by it, even, just as James was pursued by his memories. The hares couldn't outrun one another.

It had been childish folly to return to Wychcomb St. Mary. This had been the first home, the only home, he had ever known, but it hadn't ever been properly his. He had been sent here because he had nowhere else to go. And in the end, he had spent more time away at school than he ever had in the village. When the war ended, and he had nowhere to go, he let the cycle repeat, hoping the village would somehow absorb him but also cleanse him of the memories that dogged him. It was pure fantasy: his ideas about village life came more from books than they did his own experience. In truth, he was playing the role of mild-mannered country doctor as much as Leo Page played any role.

He felt adrift, unmoored, belonging to no place, belonging to no one. The only thing that was truly his own were the thoughts that plagued him.

DRESSED IN HIS TOWN clothes and reading a newspaper in an otherwise empty compartment of a London-bound train, Leo thought he might have passed as an ordinary man heading into the city for a day of work selling insurance or something equally benign. Nobody would have guessed that in his commonplace attaché case he carried a revolver, a folding knife, and a discreet capsule of cyanide. The cyanide was likely overkill for a trip to London, but Leo hardly wanted to leave it lying about his room at the Rising Sun.

When he was honest with himself—and he had long since decided that when your bread and butter was professional grade dishonesty, you had to at least make a habit of telling the truth to yourself—he admitted that he enjoyed the playacting aspect of his job. In another, kinder lifetime, he might have gone on stage. With every new assignment, he conjured a persona out of thin air. The Leonard Page who took the early train to London and dabbled in the study of church architecture might pinch his pennies, but wouldn't entertain the prospect of traveling third class. His fictional mother (widowed young, now living in someplace like Torquay, he decided) had taught him the importance of keeping up appearances, of having standards. His sister (married, three children, living in Plymouth) grew roses and had strong opinions about horticulture in general. He took his tea milky and sweet, was saving money to buy an automobile, and sometimes went to the pictures with his sweetheart.

As he looked out the window, the sun rising over the countryside, he decided that this Leonard Page would like what he saw. He'd be proud of whatever he did during the war, and would have put it behind him, or at least pretended to. Now he'd be thinking of what to get his nieces and nephews for Christmas, whether his sweetheart would prefer perfume or earrings, and whether rationing meant he wouldn't be able to get a Christmas tree.

For a moment, he had the sense that the real Leo Page might like what he saw out the train window as well, that the real Leo might like coffee rather than tea, that the real Leo might allow himself to get close to a kind-hearted country doctor. But the real Leo was a figment of his imagination, perhaps even less real than his adopted persona. He wasn't entirely sure there ever had been such a figure as the real Leo Page. That person had been left either at the orphanage or on the streets of Bristol, chased away by the mean necessities of survival. Now he was what he had been made, what he had made himself into: a tool, a weapon, a means to an end.

And yet. After gazing blankly at the newspaper for half an hour, he tossed it onto the empty seat beside him and drew his copy of *Middlemarch* from his case. Leonard Page would read no such thing. He would read the *Times*, the *New Statesman*, possibly a detective story if he were in a particularly fanciful mood. But Leo was at a good part in the book—that old sod Casaubon was finally dead—and he didn't want to put it down. He read the novel, feeling vaguely that this act of self-indulgence was the fault of Wychcomb St. Mary.

After two hours on the train, he was too restless to endure either the underground or the stuttering progress of a cab through congested streets, so he walked from Paddington Station to the building in Curzon Street. The skies were leaden gray and drooping with fog as he crossed through Hyde Park. The only other people in sight had their heads down, and scarves wrapped close around their necks as they walked quickly to wherever they had to be. Leo stopped to buy a couple of buns from a street cart, feeling sorry for the vendor who had to be out on a day like this.

He climbed the steps to the familiar building and took the rickety old lift to Templeton's floor. "I didn't catch your name last week," he said to Templeton's secretary as he placed the extra bun on her desk. He smiled in a way he imagined affable commuter Leonard Page might.

She regarded him flatly. "Mrs. Patel," she said after only the slightest hesitation to let him know that—naturally—this was not her real name, and that he was being absurd by even asking her. She flicked a glance at the bun.

"It's not poisoned," Leo protested. "I'm trying to be cordial."

"Why," she said, not bothering to make it a question. Leo felt Leonard Page disappear, a creation of smoke and mirrors; he hadn't been there in the first place. This woman likely saw agents come and go by the dozen. Half the agents who walked past this desk probably died, disappeared, or went into deep cover. Templeton had been running this operation for thirty years; surely he had a list of dead agents as long as his arm. This wasn't a normal office, where a lady in an apron would come around with a tea tray at four. They didn't even know one another's real names. It wasn't a normal office, it wasn't a normal life, and Leo would do best to remember that.

"Didn't expect to see you, Page," Templeton said when Leo walked in.

"I had to look into a few matters in town," Leo said, tamping down his inane disappointment that Templeton wasn't glad to see him. Why *should* the man be glad to see him? Leo was a good agent, a valuable asset, but he meant nothing to Templeton personally. Their relationship, such as it was, was entirely one-sided. Templeton had dozens of agents. Leo only had one Templeton, one person who had been a constant for half his life, one person he entrusted with the choice of who got to live and who didn't. He grew queasy and sank into an empty chair.

"Eh?" Templeton looked up from his papers and glanced skeptically at Leo. Leo did not know if it was his imagination or if Templeton did a double take when he saw the hand knit muffler he had looped around his neck. For one wild moment he thought Templeton was going to utter the same phrase Leo had heard from Agnes at the Rising Sun that morning, then the postmistress, and finally the stationmaster: Oh, I see you've got one of Miss Pickering's creations. Leo shoved the silly thought aside.

"You mean to tell me it's not done yet?" Templeton grumbled, not bothering to hide his irritation. "It's been nearly a week. You usually work a damned sight faster than that."

"I have the suspects narrowed down to a manageable number, sir—"

"I have MI6 breathing down my neck," Templeton barked. "Do we at least know whether this murder had anything to do with Armstrong's steel industry connections? It would be a damned relief if I knew that murder had nothing to do with whatever mischief Armstrong may or may not be up to."

"Even odds the victim was either blackmailing someone or near enough to it, which makes her a natural target for murder. But I don't know yet whether that blackmail had anything to do with Armstrong." Leo wondered if he had badly bungled the case. Ought he to have started with Armstrong's steel dealings? Had he been wasting time chatting with old ladies over milky tea?

Templeton let out an indistinct grumble.

"But if someone meant to kill her," Leo went on, mainly to fill the silence, "I can't see how it was done. How do you get the Veronal into her, I mean. If the Veronal was intended for somebody else, which is to say a guest slipped it into the glass of a dinner companion, then Mrs. Hoggett, who was fond of a tipple, might have drunk from the poisoned glass while clearing away the dinner dishes. Same for the cocktail glasses before dinner. But how would you know she had drunk it? How could you be sure? It's a bad method of murder."

Templeton grunted. "I thought the lab found no barbiturates in any of the glasses, either from the cocktails or the dinner wine."

"The glass could have been removed—slipped into a handbag, thrown out the window—and its number made up with a clean glass from the pantry." He thought of Wendy poking through the shrubbery. "But where do the stairs enter into this muddle? Did our murderer follow her up the stairs and then push her down? Or did they lure her up there? And if so, what on earth was the point of the Veronal? If they wanted her fall to look like an accident, then why do it at a time when she oughtn't to have been upstairs in the first place? At the moment she died, she ought to have been bringing the dinner dishes to the scullery. The only advantage that moment had was that all the guests and the colonel were in transit between the dining room and the drawing room at that point. Both the elderly ladies used the washroom upstairs. Norris left the room to make a phone call. The vicar went into the library to borrow a book, and Mrs. Griffiths stepped onto the terrace for a cigarette. One person could have slipped upstairs, knocked the victim on the head and shoved her down the stairs, and then run back down before the body was discovered."

"The old ladies were upstairs?" Templeton asked, and Leo thought he saw his superior's gaze dart to the muffler Leo still wore around his neck.

"They went together."

Templeton ran a hand over the bald part of his head. "Could there be two would-be murderers working independently of one another? One aiming to put Veronal in the glass of their dinner companion, the other shoving the charwoman down the stairs?"

That seemed a bit much for one dinner party, but Leo had seen stranger things, so he shrugged.

"Can we corroborate the secretary's phone call?" Templeton asked.

"There was a call from Wych Hall to London three minutes before the call to the ambulance."

"About that secretary." The older man held out a brown file folder.

Leo thumbed through the contents, his eyebrows rising steadily as he read. Edward Norris was a decorated lieutenant in the 51st Highland Division until—"Norris was a deserter?"

"Spent the rest of the war behind bars in Egypt. Armstrong would have known, of course."

Leo turned this new information over in his mind. "With a war record like that, he can't expect to find better employment. He had a solid motive in wanting to keep Armstrong alive because otherwise, he'd be out of a job." And yet—Leo flipped back through the papers on his lap—Edward Norris had listed his sister, a Lady Borthwick as his next of kin. That sounded like there was money in the family. For Norris to be working a dull job for little compensation sounded like he didn't have any recourse. Leo wondered if Norris's family had disowned him after hearing of his desertion.

Templeton tipped his head and made a skeptical sound. "Could be that Armstrong thought a deserter might be willing to look the other way while he sold military secrets. Could be that Hoggett threatened to go to the police with what she knew, and Norris didn't want to be brought up as an accomplice."

Leo rose to leave.

"Do whatever you need to do, Page. Just unpick the knot," Templeton said as Leo departed. That was what he always said: unpick the knot. As if deadly secrets could be undone in a way that resulted in smooth strands of thread. Leo knew that unpicking secrets meant unraveling a length of fabric or cutting out the secret entirely, creating a tear, a rift, a wound. That gaping absence was the cost of a secret.

That had been his first lesson. Secrets were a kind of currency. Find out the secrets of this chancellor or that industrialist, and you might be able to stop a war. Later on, he learned that those same secrets could be used to wage a war. Secrets were the invisible skeleton of society. Everything depended on the strength of secrets, and on not being able to see them; like a skeleton, once the secret was visible to the naked eye, something had gone drastically and irretrievably wrong. That was when people started to die.

Leo shivered as he stepped outside and pulled his coat tightly around him. It wasn't always Leo who did the actual killing—sometimes he simply passed on information to other people in his chain of command and let them sort out the bloody stuff. Other times he made sure the intelligence got into the hands of those who would make sure the appropriate people were punished or silenced. But after so many years of this, five of them in outright war, Leo no longer put much weight in those distinctions. His was a killing business, so he was a killer.

He slapped his hat on his head and waded through the cold and the fog to Somerset House. There were a few things he needed to confirm. When he emerged two hours later, he knew that Colonel Armstrong had a sister. Anabelle Owen, nee Armstrong, had been born in 1895. She married a fellow in the foreign service, who later became governor of some small island someplace. In 1918 she had a child, an unnamed girl, in Melbourne, Australia. Shortly thereafter, Owen died. After that, there was no record of either Anabelle or her daughter.

Armstrong was a rich man and might very well leave a legacy to his sister's child. He remembered what Mrs. Griffiths had said about how there weren't a lot of rich men who didn't have someone who wanted to kill them.

One thing was clear, and it was that Mrs. Hoggett had been too old to be Mrs. Owen's daughter. Mrs. Hoggett had been forty, and her maiden name had been Abernathy, not Owen.

When he left Somerset House, snow was beginning to fall. He wondered if the storm would reach Worcestershire this evening. He wrapped the muffler tightly around his neck and breathed in the scent of Sommers as he made his way back to Paddington Station. But the damp and cold were too much even for Sommers' muffler.

He passed a Woolworth's, its window display filled with brightly colored and foolishly festive Christmas paraphernalia. There were china figurines of Father Christmas, a couple of cards showing happy families gathered around hearths and pine trees, and packages of Christmas crackers. Without examining his thoughts, he went into the store and bought a package of a dozen crackers. He told himself that this was what Leonard Page would do. But the truth was that he had never held one in his hand, and now he wanted to. He could never know what life felt like for an ordinary person, but he could run his fingers over the same cardboard, hear the same songs, taste the same sweets. He could pretend to be the sort of person who had a life, a future, people he cared about and who cared for him in return.

He sat in his train compartment, the package of crackers on his lap, mocking him with their bright colors. He wanted to know what was inside them. He knew there would be a paper hat, and maybe a toy or a boiled sweet. He wasn't entirely certain, and that uncertainty bothered him. How had he reached nearly thirty years of age without knowing what was in Christmas crackers? That, he thought in bitter amusement, was the logical end of spycraft: needing to open the Christmas cracker a week too early.

The conductor rushed to the door of his compartment at the sound of the first cracker being opened.

"Oh, sir, you gave me a fright," the man panted. "But I suppose you're just getting a bit of a head start on the festivities?" he asked dubiously.

"Something like that." Leo pulled apart the next cracker, not flinching at the popping noise. "Care for a paper hat?"

"You ought to stop, or you'll have none left for Christmas dinner. Besides, you're supposed to open them with the person next to you."

"Oh, of course." Leo supposed he had known that, but forgotten. "Here, this'll be yours and we'll open it properly," he said, handing the remaining cracker to the conductor, who after a moment of baffled hesitation took one of the ends and pulled.

By the next station, Leo was left with a lapful of shiny foil paper, gimcrack toys, and zero intact crackers. He had unraveled his mystery and was left with nothing but trash.

WHEN JAMES GOT ON THE train, it was already nearly full of passengers coming home from London. He rejected several compartments on the grounds that they were partly occupied by noisy small children or elderly ladies who looked eager for conversation. He was about to shut the door on yet another compartment due to its occupant being apparently engaged in the process of shredding bits of foil when he realized the gentleman in question was Leo Page.

"Mr. Page? What in the name of creation are you doing?" James hadn't ever expected to see Page at a loss for words, but that was evidently the case, for Page stared at him in plain embarrassment. James peered closer at the mess on Page's lap. "Are those Christmas crackers?" To his delight, Page turned pink.

"Never mind me. I'm staging a one-man production of *The Little Match Girl.*" He swept the bits of paper into a neat pile and crammed them into his attaché case. "Terribly self-indulgent. But what are you doing?"

"Heading back to Wychcomb St. Mary, same as you."

Of course, that wasn't a good enough answer for Page. "This is one of your London days. But if you were coming from London, you wouldn't be getting on the train now. You'd have gotten on at Paddington, like me, or you would have switched to this train at Oxford. But you just got on now, at—" He looked out the window as if the passing countryside would give him any indication of the name of the station they had just left.

"Bourton on the Water," James supplied helpfully.

"The point is, not London."

"Indeed, it isn't."

Page's eyes narrowed on him with hawk like intensity. "Everyone in the village is under the impression that you go to London twice a week."

James shrugged. "Not much I can do about that."

"Are you telling me that when your patients ask where you go on Tuesdays and Thursdays, you lie to them? I can hardly credit it."

"No, I tell them the truth, which is that I have business that takes me out of town."

"And then you don't tell them why? They likely think you're up to no good."

James smiled wryly. "Nobody ever thinks I'm up to no good. I let them think whatever they want and they fill in the gaps themselves."

Page regarded him with something like admiration. "And then, eventually, they give up asking?"

"Exactly."

"And you're not going to tell me either, are you?"

James considered it. "I think if you wanted to know, you could find out in half an hour. I bet you could do it in two telephone calls."

"If you don't tell me, I'm going to assume you go to Barton on the Pond or whatever for a haircut twice a week."

James laughed. "Like Frank Churchill? I wouldn't have taken you for a Jane Austen enthusiast."

"Nobody dies in Austen," Page said, as if that were reason enough to read and enjoy something. "Nobody who appears on page, that is. She keeps all her tragedy off page," he said approvingly. "On page, it's all very much like this," he said, gesturing out the window once again at the rolling hills of the Cotswolds.

"I think that's why I came back," James said, faintly embarrassed to admit this to a man who, a week ago, had been a stranger. "I had read too much Austen and Trollope. They sold me a bill of goods."

"You ought to try *Middlemarch*. It's filled with ghastly people who still manage not to murder one another."

Page glanced down at a stray bit of shiny rubbish in his lap with a look James had often seen in field hospitals and the convalescent homes, and even more often in his own mirror. It was the look of a child who was lost at the fair and wanted nothing more than to go home, sometimes to a home that no longer existed, or never had existed in the first place.

"Do you have a family?" James asked. Page let out a grim little laugh, which James took to mean no. "Where will you be spending Christmas? We have hardly a week left. If you're still in the village, you're welcome to—"

"I'll be gone by then," Page cut in, a newly sharp tone in his voice. "Two more days at the outside."

"I see. I suppose you learned something of interest in London today?"

"Do you really want to know? Wouldn't you rather I tidy things up? Sweep all the nastier bits out of sight? It'll be like I was never here in the first place."

"No, it won't," James said.

"I suppose I've already ruined things, then?"

James shook his head. "It's true that things can't go back to how they were. There's a murderer in my village and nobody will be safe until that's dealt with. Even though I know it won't be pleasant." Saying the words aloud brought home their truth to him. "Figuring this out is important. You're doing something important."

Page stared at him, motionless except for where he rubbed the fringe of his muffler—James's muffler—between thumb and forefinger.

Chapter 9

It was high time that Leo spoke with Wendy Smythe, but the girl seemed to be in a state of perpetual motion. The gardener at Wych Hall said she had been at the kitchen door before dawn with a parcel for the housekeeper, but that he hadn't seen her since. Agnes at the Rising Sun said she had seen Wendy helping with the girl guides. The postmistress saw Wendy bringing old magazines to the vicarage for the sick children to make into garlands to festoon their tree. A rather feverish looking Mrs. Griffiths sent Wendy to the chemist, but the chemist said she had left twenty minutes earlier to bring sweets to the children at Murphy Farm. So round and round the village Leo went, chasing after a girl who apparently never sat still. Finally, he decided to go to Little Briars and wait her out. Surely she had to return home sooner or later.

Miss Pickering opened the door. "Oh. It's you." She did not look overly thrilled to find Leo on her doorstep.

"I don't suppose Wendy is here?" he asked with as charming a smile as he could manage.

The woman snorted. "She only comes home when she's on the verge of starvation or exhaustion. Like an outdoor cat, really. What did you want with her?"

Leo had come prepared with a lie. "It's about Christmas. I thought she might need an extra pair of hands to cut down trees or tack up tinsel." Is that even what one did with tinsel?

Did one tack it up or simply strew it about and hope for the best?

"She does have a bee in her bonnet about Christmas," called Miss Delacourt from the sitting room. "Come in here, Mr. Page. I have more of those ginger biscuits you liked so much the other day. And Wendy sometimes stops in for tea, so you may catch her."

Leo found Miss Delacourt sitting on the same settee she had occupied the last time he had visited. Around her shoulders was a shawl knit from fluffy wool and on her feet were a pair of embroidered slippers. He had the impression that she didn't get out much. Apart from the funeral, when she had been leaning heavily on Miss Pickering's arm, he had never seen her walk.

"I'm not sure why she's been going on about Christmas this year," Miss Pickering grumbled, sitting in the chair beside her friend. "We never made much of a production about it. Got her a new doll or a pair of ice skates."

"It was Mildred, dear. Mildred told her about the sort of Christmases your family used to have, where all the children would put on their Sunday best and go up to Wych Hall for a visit with Father Christmas and the whole pageant."

"It was ghastly," Miss Pickering said with a shudder. Leo was inclined to agree. "Some traditions are best left by the wayside."

"More honored in the breach," Miss Delacourt murmured vaguely.

"Mrs. Hoggett came from Wychcomb St. Mary?" Leo asked. That piece of information hadn't been in the dossier.

"Not exactly. Mildred was the chauffeur's daughter," said Miss Pickering. "I hadn't seen her since she was knee high. Her flat was bombed and then she was at loose ends for a number of years, so she looked me up to see if I knew of someone who needed a cleaner. I gathered she was quite desperate."

Miss Delacourt sighed. "I suppose no good deed goes unpunished." Miss Pickering shot her a quelling glance.

"Her mother was the cook," Miss Pickering reminisced. "Mildred lived here until her father died, and then her mother ran off with the under butler. Goodness, it's lowering to remember how grand a place Little Briars was."

"No place is grand anymore," Miss Delacourt said, inexpertly winding a ball of yarn. "Unless it's owned by an actor, in which case it's floor to ceiling gilt. Oh, but back in our day, which wasn't so very long ago, even the most modest establishment had a dozen servants at least. And they all had uniforms, like that girl up at Wych Hall." She looked directly at Leo. "I thought that was a very nice touch," she added, dropping her voice to a confiding tone. "Exactly what that sort of man would want. I do hope he doesn't bother her. That, I'm afraid, is a risk of the job."

Miss Delacourt looked on the verge of continuing, but Miss Pickering cut her off. "Cora," she said, a note of warning in her voice. "Mr. Page doesn't want to hear about the perils of being a parlor maid."

"I do wander," Miss Delacourt admitted. "But now you have me thinking of the old days. Mr. Page, would you like to hear about a very large hat?"

Leo suspected this was a maneuver to distract him from asking about Mildred Hoggett. But he couldn't very well insist that they cough up whatever secrets they were hiding. So he made a murmur of interest.

"Oh, no, Cora," Miss Pickering said, grabbing the lumpy mass of yarn out of the other lady's hands and regarding it balefully. "Not that story."

Leo had the sense that even in this overheated sitting room, they were surrounded by secrets, that any conversational gambit was straying into forbidden territory. He felt at once disoriented and oddly at home. He knew the rules of this game, where both parties jealously guarded their secrets while simultaneously pretending they had none. And with two elderly ladies, the secrets couldn't be so bad.

"I insist," Miss Delacourt said. "This is just the sort of story to amuse Mr. Page. It was at a house party, one of those things people did before the war. Before the first war, I mean. A house filled with guests and servants, four changes of clothing a day. I had to go to immense trouble with scarves and bits of trim to disguise the fact that I only had fourteen dresses, although now looking back fourteen is a frightful lot, isn't it, Edith?"

"Frightful," Miss Pickering agreed. "I believe I brought four trunks of clothing for that party. And two French maids, one to attend to my wardrobe and the other to do my hair. But Mr. Page doesn't want to hear about your dresses. If you're going to tell this awful story, you might as well get to the part about the shooting."

Leo's ears pricked up at the word shooting. He had expected a meandering tale about cats or horses or whatever it was old ladies talked about. He hadn't realized firearms were to be involved.

"Oh dear. I told you, I'm too inclined to ramble. It happens at my age. So, this party was at Lord Listerdale's place in Kent and it rained five days straight. The gentlemen went out riding, but of course the ladies had to stay indoors, which was very tedious. In the evenings, we played charades and all those parlor games that are nothing but excuses for young people to grope one another. I don't mind telling you that by the end I was quite bored of being pawed at and proposed to."

"And rightly so," Miss Pickering said firmly, but she was smiling down at her yarn.

"Well, on the sixth day, there was sun and we all went a bit mad. We had a picnic and the champagne flowed quite freely. Of course, at the time one knew these parties were expensive but looking back I quite shudder at what the wine alone must have cost. It's probably indecent, what with starving children and so forth. But that's neither here nor there. One of the gentlemen—I think it was the youngest son of the Duke of Somerset—was very rich and wild and nobody dared say 'what is wrong with you, Harold, waving a pistol around at a picnic with ladies about,' but we were all thinking it, I assure you. So, not wanting to get shot, I dared him to shoot an apple off the fence post. The idea, you see, was to have him shoot in quite another direction," the old lady said. "Away from people."

"Very clever of you," Leo said. And it was clever. It's what he would have done in the same situation. Again, he had the disorienting sense of being in his element—that despite the bric-a-brac and the chintz, he was as at home here as he would be in a safe house in Minsk or an armaments warehouse in Toulouse.

"Of course, he fired quite wide of the mark. But the other gentlemen felt compelled as a matter of honor to try as well, gentlemen being what they are, and drunken gentlemen even more so. The trouble was that now at least three gentlemen had pistols waving about in the breeze. Thinking quickly, I said that I bet I could shoot the apple myself. I insisted that they all lay their weapons on the grass so nobody could say one of the gentlemen had shot the apple for me in a fit of gallantry. And of course, they all did, thinking they were humoring me."

"Men did whatever Cora told them to, the idiots," Miss Pickering muttered.

"I shot the apple, and then I shot a lime, then a conker, and I'm afraid I got a bit carried away with my own skill. The rest of the story does me no credit."

Miss Pickering snorted as Miss Delacourt's crepey cheeks blushed pink.

"Well, Edith had on the most magnificent hat. Birds in a nest, flowers on the vine, positively teeming with flora and fauna. And somebody bet five crowns that I could shoot one of the birds perched on the top of her hat. And, well, that's exactly what I did!" She ended her narrative with a sheepish smile.

"It was my favorite hat," Miss Pickering remarked.

"You shot at your friend?" Leo was very nearly aghast. He hadn't known he was still capable of shock, but the idea of Miss Delacourt with her fluffy white hair and badly wound wool engaging in this lunatic behavior was too outrageous. This story, for all it had been dressed up with champagne and dukes and elaborate hats, did not belong in a polite drawing room any more than he did. Either this story was a fabrication or Miss Delacourt had been an absolute bedlamite as a girl. Leo had more than decent aim and he wouldn't have risked shooting anywhere near an innocent person unless it was a matter of necessity.

"Oh dear, now I've scandalized our guest. It was most imprudent of me, I know, but there was no real risk—you young people cannot imagine how massive hats were in those days—which of course Edith knew, which was why she agreed to it."

"Nonsense. I agreed to it because I wanted you to put those men in their places."

"I ought to have held out for more than five crowns, though. I did have to eat. Impecunious ladies couldn't simply get a job in those days. And I was not cut out to be a governess."

"Certainly not," Edith said.

Leo laughed. He couldn't help it. "I think you're all mad," he managed. "Positively barking." And for a moment he felt like it wasn't Leo Page, fictitious enthusiast of church architecture, who was speaking, but rather some authentic version of himself that he hadn't yet realized existed, and he knew he had to get out of here before that person emerged again.

Wendy still had not returned, and he couldn't stretch this visit out without seeming suspicious, so he rose to his feet to leave. But when he stood, he realized he had unconsciously taken hold of one of the skeins of wool in Miss Pickering's basket and wound it into a perfectly neat sphere.

JAMES WAS FINISHING up his rounds during his second weekly visit to the nursing home when he thought he heard an oddly familiar voice. Rather, the voice wasn't just familiar but also out of context, a voice that belonged somewhere else.

He followed the sound down a corridor into the room of Mr. Dempsey, one of the sadder cases in this establishment. Mr. Dempsey had suffered a head injury during one of the war's later campaigns and hadn't fully recovered. In fact, his recovery hardly even deserved the term: he could neither talk nor read, and there were entire weeks when he failed to respond to speech. When James entered his room, he saw Dempsey propped up in a chair, looking out the window, as he did most days.

Beside him was Edward Norris.

James knew he ought to clear his throat, knock on the open door, or do anything to let his presence be known. But he was so struck by the alteration in Norris that he could hardly bring himself to move. The secretary had always seemed cold and sneaky, but now he was talking animatedly to Dempsey.

"The place is a drafty old pile, but we've seen worse, haven't we? The food is damned good. I can't really complain." Norris paused, as if giving the other man time to respond. "That's right, old man, lucky to have the spot, I daresay. Don't really know what I'd do otherwise."

Dempsey remained impassive, staring as ever out the window.

"Is that a letter from your sister? I'll read it to you." Norris tore open the envelope. "Good God, long-winded as ever, Frannie is. Four sheets of paper, front and back. Surely the old girl knows you can't read yet."

That *yet* made James's stomach clench. The groundless optimism of it, the casual cheer.

"Well I'm dashed if I'm going to read the whole thing," Norris went on. "I'll give you the salient details. Ah, she's had the baby. It's a boy and Markham is over the moon, as one would expect. The child is hale and hearty and quite fat and—" He broke off with a strangled noise, then recovered himself. "Looks like they're naming the kid after you. I say, that's awfully good." He flipped through the remaining pages and then put them back in the envelope. "I read in the paper that my sister had another brat. She and Borthwick would crawl over hot coals before acknowledging that I'm the proud uncle, let alone naming the poor thing after me. Jesus Christ." He pinched the bridge of his nose. "Ah, well, that was the whole point of the thing, wasn't it?" Norris lapsed into silence and James backed away.

After turning a corner, James leaned against the wall and composed himself. That was a side of Norris he hadn't ever seen. Hadn't wanted to see, if he were honest. If Mildred Hoggett had been murdered, he wanted to believe that Norris, the person at that dinner party he liked least, had been responsible. But surely even murderers did good deeds. Even murderers visited the sick, even those too sick to know they had visitors. Even murderers could get teary-eyed at the news of a friend's new nephew. But that scene had rearranged James's notions of Norris.

He found the nurse who was on duty. "Sister Reynolds, who is that man with Mr. Dempsey? He looks familiar."

"The handsome, fair fellow? That's Edwin Nesbitt, an army friend of the poor man. He visits once a week, like clockwork."

James digested the fact that Norris was using an assumed name. "I've never seen him."

"His usual day is Sunday, Dr. Sommers. I couldn't say why he came today instead."

James thanked her and proceeded to the office of the nursing home's administrator, a small, dark man in wire-rimmed spectacles. After a preamble of small talk about weather and golf, James cleared his throat. "I've been looking into foundations that provide for patients who might need permanent nursing," he said, trying not to blush at the lie. "And it occurred to me that our Mr. Dempsey might be eligible."

"Dempsey?" the administrator said. "He'll certainly need nursing for the rest of his life, barring a miracle, but he's quite well provided for. My impression is that his parents are rather well-heeled. They arrive in an enormous Rolls Royce."

"They visit often?"

"Weekly. So do his sisters. They all fairly dote on him."

As James walked to the station and boarded the train that would take him home, he wondered two things. First, why on earth had Norris been using a false name? Second, what had he meant when he said, "that was the point of the whole thing" in reference, presumably, to his estrangement from his sister. It hinted at a skeleton in Norris's closet, an idea that James found darkly comforting. God, if only it really could be that simple. If the blame lay with Norris—a stranger, an interloper—then maybe James would know some peace.

Chapter 10

Leo finally found Wendy Smythe in the graveyard, propped up against a headstone that faced the bare patch of earth under which Mildred Hoggett had been buried earlier that week. She was wearing what appeared to be men's trousers, a pair of ancient wellingtons, and a pea coat that had seen better days. Her head was bare, revealing a pair of black plaits that didn't seem to have been combed any time recently. In one hand she had a battered steel flask.

"Is this a private party?" he asked, sitting on the headstone next to Mrs. Hoggett's grave. He had his sketchbook and a few sharp pencils in case he needed to look busy. "I've been looking for you since yesterday. Led me a merry chase, didn't you?"

"Oh, hello. I ought to remember who you are, oughtn't I?"

"Leo Page," he said. "I saw you at the vicarage after the funeral, and then in passing at Little Briars, but we weren't introduced." The girl's eyes barely focused on him. "Are you very drunk or is there any hope of me catching up?"

"I'm not drunk at all, more's the pity. I'm just sort of working myself up to it. It's gin, though, and very nasty. Would you like some?"

"No thank you," he said politely, tamping down an uncharacteristic urge to snatch the flask out of her hand. Surely fifteen-year-old girls should not be drinking out of flasks in the middle of the day. "But if you'd like to come with me to the Rising Sun, I'll stand you a pint. It'll be warmer and less damp than a graveyard. You're probably chilled to the skin. But if you'd rather stay out here and you don't mind company, I have to sketch this side of the church."

"Early perpendicular," Wendy said with an air of great authority.

"Are you quite certain you aren't drunk?"

"Dead sober. Early perpendicular Gothic. That's what the church is."

"Duly noted. It's a large church for a village this size."

"Wychcomb St. Mary used to be quite the place round about 1400 or so. Quite the thriving metropolis." She took a tentative sip of the gin, wincing. "And no, I don't want to go to the pub. I'm committed to discomfort. There's room on this headstone for two." She shifted over a few inches, and Leo sat on the grass beside her. "Besides, you're maybe the third person to come talk to me today. I shouldn't leave. What if somebody else pays me a visit and I'm not here to receive them? Rude."

"Who else has been here?"

"James stopped by on his way from the train station to the church. And Sally Bright passed me on the way to the post office." With apparent effort, she turned her head to face him. "Mr....whoever you are, no don't tell me, it'll just fall out again. Did you know you can leave a person money just to make mischief for them?"

Leo raised his eyebrows. "A nasty trick. Did that happen to you?"

"I have no idea, more's the pity. She—" Wendy gestured broadly at the grave opposite them "—left me a bit of money. And I don't know whether she did it out of kindness or because she wanted to make trouble for me. Which is dashed irritating, because I don't know whether to remember her as friend or foe, and that sort of thing wreaks havoc on the brain."

"How is the money making trouble for you," Leo asked, trying not to sound as curious as he was.

"Because the lawyer says that I'll need to prove that I'm Wendy Smythe. Mrs. Hoggett knew I'd be able to do no such thing."

"Are you Wendy Smythe?" Leo asked mildly.

"Of course I am, you ninny. But I haven't any papers saying so."

Sommers had told Leo that the vicar's wife claimed to have lost them, which sounded like the purest claptrap. "You say Mrs. Hoggett knew this?"

"She's the one who told me!"

"Told you what?"

"That Mary fudged the whole thing."

"How so?" It was not pleasant to think of, but Mary Griffiths was just barely old enough to have a fifteen-year-old daughter.

"Oh, my mother was useless. Always leaving me alone in the flat and going off with men after my dad died. I don't remember much, but I do remember that. I suppose somebody took pity on me and called upon Mary to find me a better home, as one would do with an ill-treated kitten," she concluded miserably.

"You'll beg my pardon, but I've met Mrs. Griffiths. If I wanted anything done at all, she's the last person on earth I'd ask for help. Yesterday she had on a pair of mismatched stockings. I'd hardly trust her to spirit away a neglected child."

That got a sleepy smile out of the girl. "That *is* reassuring." Then her brow furrowed. "But you see, she's just the person who *would* forget to arrange for proper paperwork."

Leo decided it was time for a different line of inquiry before the child fell asleep. "Did you find what you were looking for in the shrubbery at Wych Hall the other evening?"

Wendy stared blearily at him for a moment. "I have no idea what you're talking about."

"I'm not asking what you were looking for. That doesn't matter right now. But if it gets about that you're doing some amateur sleuthing, you might not be safe."

"If I were a more sensitive type, I might be quite cast down. Who *are* you?"

"A benevolent spirit?" he suggested, deciding not to even pretend to give a direct answer. "Like the elves and the shoemaker."

"Is that what you were doing in James's house the other night? Making shoes?"

He took the flask from her hand and made a show of screwing the cap on tightly before handing it back to her. "We played gin rummy and discussed church architecture."

"Wendy! What in heaven's name are you doing?"

Leo turned to see Miss Pickering standing over them. Had she followed Leo from Little Briars?

"Talking to Mr. Page," Wendy said with a yawn. She rose unsteadily to her feet, supported by Leo's arm.

"I do have eyes and I can see as much," Miss Pickering said, flicking a critical glance over both of them. "I meant what are you doing in the graveyard. You'll catch your death, sitting on the ground like that. Come now. I'll take you back to the house and get you warmed up. But first, I need to take this greenery into the church. They're meant to be decorating for Christmas." She had an armful of ivy and holly.

"I can take those in for you, Miss Pickering," Leo offered. "I think Wendy needs a nap."

Wendy stuck her tongue out at him, but made her slightly tottering way out of the graveyard. Miss Pickering deposited the greenery into Leo's arms and then narrowed her eyes. "I think it's time for your holiday to end, Mr. Page." Then she nodded her head once and then turned to follow Wendy toward the path that led to Little Briars.

His arms loaded with greenery, he went through the front door of the church, where he was immediately pounced upon by a middle-aged lady who divested him of the leaves. In exaggeratedly hushed whispers, she thanked him profusely before bustling off in the direction of what Leo assumed was the vestry or wherever they kept those enormous brass pots for flowers and such.

He took a deep breath, inhaling the scent of lemon furniture polish and candle wax, but it struck him as incomplete. He had come to England as a child and had never really thought of himself as a Catholic, but it still struck him as vaguely debased that the churches here tended not to use incense. This, he supposed, was as close to a religious conviction as he was ever going to develop. He had no inclination to linger in this foreign, wrong-smelling house of worship, and was about to turn on his heel and leave when he spotted Sommers. He was sitting about ten pews back from the altar, by all appearances deep in thought or prayer. Leo could slip in beside him, flirt, and finagle an invitation to the doctor's house later that night. On the other hand, every minute Leo spent with Sommers made it harder to see the case clearly. Or, no: he could see perfectly clearly, but he didn't want to, because the picture that was starting to take shape in his mind was not at all something Sommers would like in the least bit.

He carefully picked a holly leaf off his coat. He'd smell like yuletide cheer for days and resented it bitterly. Maybe it was the Christmas scent, maybe it was the ecclesiastical surroundings, or maybe it was just the solid presence of the man in the pew a few yards away, but for a moment Leo wondered what it would be like in a world where he could fill his days with things that were good and sweet and uncomplicated. He'd like to spend a few days in bed with James, but also having tea and doing crosswords and whatever else people did when they weren't Leo Page.

"I see you've come to examine the Three Hares from the inside," Sommers said, having come up beside him while Leo was lost in thought.

Leo followed the other man's gaze to the window on the wall behind the altar. It was three rabbits or hares, chasing one another in a circle, and arranged so that their three visible ears formed a sort of triangle in the center. You couldn't tell which ears belonged to which hare. No, Leo thought, looking at the window with narrowed eyes, that wasn't it at all. Each hare had two ears, but it shared an ear with each of its neighbors. If you thought about it too long you were liable to have your eyes cross. He had seen this sort of optical illusion before. In the southeast of England, they were called Tinners' Rabbits for some reason, but they turned up in churches in parts of France and Germany, too, and Leo had a dim memory of something similar on the wall of the church the sisters had brought the orphans to three times a week.

"Why three?" Leo asked, struck by the thought. "You could do the same trick with ten rabbits. Or even with two."

"Past, present, and future. The holy trinity. Rebirth. Salvation." He sounded almost wistful.

Leo rather thought it was dismal, this endless circle, but far be it from him to piss on another man's comfort.

"I need to ask you something," Leo started, then shook his head. He wasn't going to question Sommers. Any answer Sommers could give, Page could find out from another source, and asking him would only create an opportunity for lies. And when Page looked back on this case, he didn't want to remember that he had made James Sommers lie. "Can I buy you dinner? Is there anywhere to eat other than the Rising Sun?" It was too many questions all at once, a sure sign of nervousness, and Leo wanted to kick himself.

James opened his mouth and snapped it shut, then ran his hands through his hair. It was as if they were having a nervous habit contest. "The Rising Sun is fine."

JAMES HAD NEVER BEEN a reckless child. Other boys had gotten up to trouble, but whenever James thought about what fun he might have sneaking out after dark or stealing ripe fruit from the neighbor's orchard, he weighed it against the inconvenience it would cause his uncle. His increasingly infrequent letters from his mother always pointedly reminded him of the great kindness his uncle had bestowed on him by taking him in, and James had never let himself forget it. His uncle never said a word about it, and sometimes even seemed to enjoy having James about, but James had heard the whispers in the village: the vicar was such a good man, such a kind man, to do his duty by the son of his unfortunate nephew. And James figured that if Uncle Henry wanted James to spend a summer's day cataloging his index instead of frolicking with the other lads, the least James could do was oblige him.

Now, sitting across a table from Leo Page, he felt the same sense of guilty anticipation he might have had as an adventurous boy. He tried to remind himself that it was a terrible idea to let himself care for a man like Page, if for no other reason than that Page would soon be leaving. But as he looked at Page, he felt like a man slipping in and out of a dream, in and out of a world where Page belonged here, with him.

As they ate, Page heartily digging into a pork pie and James distractedly picking at his own, no fewer than six people greeted Page by name.

"You work fast," James remarked. He meant it as a commentary on Page's charm, and only realized after the words had left his mouth that wheedling his way into people's lives was indeed Page's work. He felt his cheeks heat, but Page gave him a half smile and raised his glass.

"I'm irresistible," Page said, and James felt his cheeks heat even more.

"Who do you think did it?" he asked, then watched as Page's face shifted into a cautious mask. It had been the wrong thing to say. Any hope of easy flirtation was quite gone now.

"James," Page said, and it was the first time either of them had used first names. James might have liked it more if it had happened a few minutes earlier. "It had to have been someone at that dinner party. Armstrong or his secretary. Wendy. The vicar or his wife. The two old ladies. The housemaid. That's eight people. The simplest explanation is that Mrs. Hoggett found something out about one of them and needed to be silenced."

"Right," James said. "But what do you think she found out?"

"Colonel Armstrong could have any number of secrets," he said vaguely. "Or perhaps she found out what skeletons Mr. Norris has in his closet. She might have discovered the truth of Wendy's background. Could Mrs. Hoggett have found out that Wendy's natural father is walking around the village? Say, the colonel himself? Or the vicar?"

James had been poised to tell Page what he had seen in the nursing home that afternoon, but the mention of Wendy brought him up short. "Griffiths? Come now."

"It would explain why he and his wife brought the girl here. And surely you're aware that the Griffiths children look rather like Wendy."

James had noticed the resemblance only the other day. But surely pale, freckled skin and unruly dark hair were common enough characteristics. He pushed the thought from his mind. "I can't see Griffiths or Mary committing murder to conceal the existence of an illegitimate child. All right, which other of my friends has sinister secrets?" He aimed for a jesting tone and failed miserably.

"Mildred Hoggett's father was the chauffeur for the Pickering family. She may have known something about Miss Pickering or even Miss Delacourt. The two of them seem to have been thick as thieves for decades."

James did not know whether Page spoke these last words with particular emphasis or if he only imagined it. He had long assumed that the ladies at Little Briars were more than old companions, but the idea of them being blackmailed over the nature of their friendship was outrageous. "They're both past seventy. What kind of secrets would they bother killing for at this point in their lives? Cora was notorious in her youth. I can't imagine anyone being surprised at any scandal she had been tied up in. If one of them had a secret baby or a married lover, it wouldn't matter."

Page blinked. "You're assuming that sexual scandal is the only kind of secret a woman can have." He took a long sip of his ale. "Another possibility is that Mrs. Hoggett wasn't the intended victim. Perhaps the Veronal was intended for someone else, and Mrs. Hoggett simply had to be killed because otherwise, she'd be able to say whose glass she drank from."

James shook his head. "Are you certain you aren't reading too much into this? Maybe your, ah, training has made you look for explanations more elaborate than the situation calls for."

"Are you certain your own background hasn't led you to hide important details from me?" Page asked levelly. "I'm not holding it against you," he added magnanimously. Before James could object, Page broke into a broad smile. "I do like you despite your vast innocence."

James felt the tips of his ears heat. "There is something I ought to tell you," he admitted. "But I don't want to."

"Ah," Page said, his gaze flicking away over James's shoulder, his smile cooling by several degrees.

"Not because I mistrust you or because I want to thwart your enquiries," James added hastily. "But because I'd rather—oh blast it. Can't we have supper and spend a couple of hours together without thinking of horrible things? I just...I want that, Page. Leo. I promise that I'll tell you later. Or, um, tomorrow?" Now his entire face was hot as he blushed at his own obviousness—he might as well have announced his intentions to go to bed with Page that night.

But Page only gave him a small smile. "A difficulty in my line of work is that it's difficult to have a proper getting-to-know-you conversation without invoking the Official Secrets Act. For instance, right now I'd like to ask you where you went to school and whether you lost anyone in the war, but I wouldn't be able to give you anything honest in return."

James furrowed his brow. "Don't you think there's more to who we are than what we do? I think I could tell you who I am without giving any actual details about my life."

"Give it a try," Page said, plainly skeptical.

"I'm a—no, wait." He had been about to say that he was a doctor, that he lived in a small village, but those were the sorts of details that Page couldn't reciprocate. He tried to think of what was at the core of who he was, the drive that led him to make the choices he had made. Why was he a doctor? Why did he live in this village? "I like being useful." The words sounded incredibly small, so much less but also so much more than *I'm a doctor.* "I like having a place where I belong. I see the same people every day, and we have endless iterations of the same conversations, and I don't find it boring in the least. It's soothing."

An odd expression stole across Page's face, and then vanished as quickly as it had appeared. "Here, let me try. I was born near the French border." James noticed he didn't say which border, an omission that could only be deliberate. "I—oh, devil take it, I'm very bad at honesty. Sommers, I cannot think of a single damned thing to say that isn't either a lie or a felony." His voice was low, and James leaned close to hear him. "I like birds. I like this ugly muffler. I like you and I keep catching myself daydreaming that I'm somebody else, somebody who could spend time with you. There. How's that?"

James swallowed. "That's very good indeed."

They sat in silence for a moment, James faintly dazed and Page with barely contained energy. James knew that look. He saw it in patients sometimes, both in the village and in London, that urge to confess, to lay bare your soul. He guessed Leo Page had plenty to confess, and for a moment James wanted to hear it all, even though anything Page had to confess would have to be very bad indeed.

Then they were interrupted. "Dr. Sommers!" A young woman James recognized as the housemaid at Wych Hall approached their table. "Come quick. Colonel Armstrong has been shot!"

Chapter 11

Hell and bother. There went the simplest explanation for what had been going on at Wych Hall. Sally Bright, very competently playing the part of a frightened girl, confirmed that an ambulance and the police had already been summoned. She had come to the Rising Sun to tell Leo of the murder, but when she saw him with James, she thought fast, making it seem like she had come for the doctor. Leo resolved to commend her to Templeton.

"Do you have a car?" Leo asked James, who seemed to be having a hard time shrugging into his overcoat. Leo held the coat to make it easier for the doctor to put on, and noticed that the man's hands were shaking. "I'll drive you," Leo offered. James was in no condition to drive, and Leo wanted an excuse to go to Wych Hall and see what happened.

They got there in five minutes, Sally in the back seat, and Leo going as fast as James's little car could take them. While they had been at the Rising Sun, the snow Leo had seen in London had finally reached Worcestershire, but it wasn't falling heavily enough yet to slow his progress on the road. On the gravel drive of Wych Hall, he brought the car to a skidding halt. There was no sign yet of an ambulance or the police, for which Leo was grateful. He wanted to see the state of things before they were interfered with.

Inside, the housekeeper led them to the library. Colonel Armstrong sat at his desk, his cheek resting on the blotting paper in a small pool of blood. His eyes were open, staring vacantly in the direction of the door, and in the center of his forehead was a neat red hole.

"Damnation," Leo said. "I don't think we need the ambulance after all."

But James went to the body all the same and checked for a surely nonexistent pulse. "Nothing to be done. He's still warm," James said, sounding far away. "Dead less than an hour, I'd say, but the medical examiner will have to confirm."

"Did you hear the shot?" Leo asked the housekeeper.

"Certainly not."

"Did you hear anything at all? You might have thought it was a car having trouble or a poacher in the wood."

"I heard nothing," Mrs. Clemens repeated, then pursed her lips. "You may ask Sally Bright whether she heard any odd noises, but she and I were the only ones in the house."

"Where's Norris?" Leo asked.

"He went to London this morning. I expected him back for dinner, but he wired this afternoon and said not to expect him back until tomorrow," the housekeeper said.

Leo had to suppress a hysterical laugh. If this murder had been done to demolish his favorite explanation, it couldn't have been more thorough. He went to James, seeing that the man looked a bit unsteady. He put a hand on the doctor's shoulder. "Why don't we get out of this room," he suggested. There was nothing to be gained by staying with the body. "We'll have to tell the police what we saw, but then you can go home."

There would be no getting rid of the police this time. A man shot clean in the middle of his forehead was not something that could be dismissed as an accidental death. He was struck by the idea that Mrs. Hoggett's death had been caused by two events that separately could have been chalked up as accidents—an overdose of sleeping powder followed by a tumble down the stairs. Armstrong's death, on the other hand, was arranged in a way that could only be murder. Leo didn't know if that meant the killer had changed tactics or if there were two different minds at work. But if one thing was clear, it was that the local police, and likely Scotland Yard, were going to be all over the place. Templeton would be furious.

James gave a quick nod of his head, his jaw clenched. Leo steered him out of the room to the great hall and almost pushed him bodily onto a bench. Then he went back into the library and examined it more thoroughly than he had before. Everything looked much as it had when he had visited a few days earlier. The windows were locked, but the french doors weren't. Using his handkerchief, he gingerly opened the doors. The snow was now an inch deep and the body had been dead for probably an hour. There was no hope of finding any footprints, even though the murder had almost certainly been committed after the snow had begun falling. He noticed a few drops of water on the wood floor between the french doors and the desk. It could be melted snow, but too little to be explained by a person entering through the french doors with snow stuck to the soles of their shoes. Then he left the library, shutting the door and turning the key in the lock behind him.

"Is there anything I can get you?" He sat beside James, who was still white-faced and ragged looking. "Could you manage some tea?" The bench was hard, one of those decorative bits of furniture that get shoved against empty walls. He wished there was somewhere more comfortable he could take James, but right now he needed to keep an eye on the door to the library.

"I could smell the blood." James's voice was ragged.

Leo nodded. He had smelled it too. There hadn't been that much of it, at least, because the colonel had died quickly. "Bad memories?" he asked.

James shuddered. "Something like that. Awful reaction for a doctor to have. Rather hard to do surgery when you can't abide the sight of blood."

Oh, damn. Leo hadn't realized. "Is that what sets you off? Blood?"

"Blood always sets me off. It's not the blood itself so much as the sense of people being...flesh."

Leo didn't understand, and his face must have shown it because James continued.

"I think of how the war changed people into bodies. Flesh that had to be stitched together, meat that had to be dug through to find bullets. Anything that reminds me of that sets me off. Makes my brain play an infinite newsreel of my most gruesome memories." He ran a hand through his hair. "I don't talk much about it. Most people wouldn't understand. They'd think I was off my head."

He heard the police cars on the gravel drive; otherwise, he might have been tempted to take James in his arms. As that wasn't an option, he patted James's leg and went to answer the door.

BY THE TIME THE POLICE were done questioning them repeatedly about the events of that evening, the clock had struck two, the housekeeper had produced innumerable cups of tea, and James felt like something inside him had broken into a thousand pieces. He knew he was fragile, dammit; he knew things like blood and violence were all too liable to set him off. But he was usually able to put himself back together again, or at least to produce a reasonable simulacrum of sanity. Now he just wanted to go home, lock the door behind him, and barricade himself against the foul truth of what evils people could do to one another.

This summer an elderly patient of his died. He had been sad, he had been sorry, and he had experienced a small shudder of horror at the sight of the lifeless body. But that had been a natural death. Colonel Armstrong had died in a grossly unnatural way, not from disease, or time, or even a motor accident, but by the hand of another person. It was too similar to the many deaths he had witnessed during the war, a realization that set off another round of dizziness and nausea.

He closed his eyes and tried to fill his lungs with air, tried to root his body in the present, but he thought he could still make out the metallic scent of blood even though the body had long since been removed.

Except for a few minutes when Leo had quietly spoken to the chief constable, he hadn't left James's side since the police arrived. He had even given James a few pats on the leg, such an awkward attempt at consolation that James might have laughed at any other time. But he had stayed, and he hadn't said anything awful—he hadn't urged James to buck up or get on with it or any of the other things people were wont to say to a man in the middle of one of these episodes. James had heard doctors and nurses at the nursing home say that sort of thing to patients, and had vowed never to inflict such a load of bollocks on anyone in his care. And now he was unspeakably grateful that Leo, whoever he was, whatever he was, whatever deceitful intrigue he was up to, had the kind of tact or instinct that saw him through this kind of situation.

"I'm going to take the doctor home now," Leo announced with an air of authority that ought to have clued anyone in to the fact that he wasn't a shipping clerk on holiday. "He has to do his rounds in the morning." James, through the foggy jumble of his brain, gathered that Leo had let his disguise drop, but before he could consider the implications, Leo was casually steering him out the door and into the car.

"What usually helps?" Leo asked, after they were on the road, Leo once again driving. "Do you have pills or powders or something?"

Of course, he did. He had all those things in his surgery. "Nothing that'll leave me fit for my duties tomorrow."

"Do the pills help?"

"They...end it. Temporarily." The mention of pills reminded him of something, but his mind was too wooly to remember what. "But they won't do me any good right now. The initial shock is over, and I only need time and peace to get my head on straight." That wasn't the entire truth. Barbiturates were a godsend for putting one out of one's misery on a temporary basis. Of course, a miscalculation in dose could end one's troubles rather too permanently. And the unwanted effects—torpor, nausea, tremor, confusion—were often just as bad as the episode itself. Moreover, they didn't prevent the next occurrence. It was dread of the next time, the knowledge that he'd be dealing with these recurrences for years or forever, that depressed James the most.

He had wondered if that was why his father had ended his own life. When his uncle spoke of it, he simply said James's father wasn't right in the head, poor man. That had seemed an adequate explanation to James as a child; surely, a man would only commit suicide if he wasn't right in his head. And he still agreed, more or less. But now he had known and treated so many people who weren't right in their head—and at the moment he had to admit he wasn't quite right in his head himself—who hadn't had the faintest interest in suicide. And he had seen otherwise rational people die by their own hand. He thought, though, that he now understood the grinding, never ending cycle of trauma that could make death seem like the only option.

"I'm not going to shoot myself," he said, and only realized he had said it aloud when Leo responded.

"Good thing, that," Leo said easily, as if they were talking about the weather or horse races or something equally inconsequential. "Thank you for letting me know."

"I didn't mean to say that aloud."

"Glad you did. I was working up to asking you delicately and you've saved me the trouble." He turned the car into James's drive and parked it expertly.

"What did you tell them?" James asked, as Leo took the latchkey from his hand and unlocked the front door. "The police, I mean. What did you say to make them listen to you?"

"I told them I was a visiting specialist from the Home Office."

"Oh, the Home Office. I hadn't realized." He had thought military, but Home Office made sense as well.

"I'm not," Page said tightly. But his hand was gentle on the small of James's back as he ushered him inside.

"How does it work?" James asked as Leo helped him out of his coat. Really, he could manage this on his own. He wasn't that far gone. But it felt nice to have someone's hands on him. "Aren't you afraid that you'll be exposing Irish bombers next month and someone will recognize you as the Home Office, church window fellow from Wychcomb St. Mary?"

"No, that's not how it works. First, I don't spend much time in any single place. Second, I'm rather average looking—"

James snorted, and was surprised he was capable of even the faintest display of mirth.

"No, I am. I'm well aware of my own charms," he added with a wry smile, "but there's nothing about me that stands out. If I put on a sailor's uniform, then I'm a sailor. If I wear a tweed jacket and shabby corduroy trousers—" he gestured to his current ensemble "—then I'm a London clerk spending a holiday in the country."

James didn't like the idea that the Leo he saw before him wasn't authentic, but he had always known that. He was distracted by Leo's hands on his arms, turning him toward the wall. Leo pulled the overcoat from James' shoulders and hung it on a hook near the door. Then, after a moment of hesitation, he took off his own coat and hung it beside James's.

"I ought to have brought you to Little Briars," Leo murmured, his hand still on the hook.

"Why?"

"I don't like the idea of you being alone right now."

James bristled. "I don't need nursing. I'm a doctor."

"I've heard doctors make the worst patients."

"And I already told you I'm not going to do anything stupid."

"I know that. What I'm saying is that I don't want to leave you alone, and the ladies at Little Briars would probably do a better job taking care of you than I will."

"You're staying?" James asked, befuddled.

"We were at Wych Hall half the night and nobody could expect me to wake up poor Agnes at the Rising Sun to let me in at this hour. Besides, your car is the only one in the drive, and I'll be out of here bright and early, so your reputation will be untarnished."

James hadn't been thinking of his reputation, only of how Leo's presence would not do anything to soothe his rattled mind. The man James was—no use mincing words—falling for wasn't even real. It was all battle camouflage. And the last thing on earth James needed was another reminder of war.

But when Leo led him up the stairs and into the bedroom, James went docilely. He let Leo strip him down to singlet and shorts and lay him in bed. He watched as Leo seemed to deliberate, glancing between the chair by the window and the half empty bed. James, his limbs weak after the events of that night, languidly patted the bed beside him. Finally, Leo kicked off his shoes and climbed into bed. James couldn't have said whether he moved to Leo or if it was the other way around, but his back was soon against Leo's chest, one of Leo's arms tucked snugly around him.

LEO WAS TOO ACCUSTOMED to waking up in odd places and indeed with surprising companions that he didn't need more than a few seconds to recall whose bed he was in, whose warm body pressed beside his side. He allowed himself to linger for the space of a few heartbeats, allowed himself to acknowledge that in another lifetime he might have found a way to stay. But in this world, he didn't have the luxury of long mornings with lovely men. With a sense of grim resignation, he extracted himself from James's embrace and crept downstairs, where he used the telephone in the surgery to call Templeton's secretary.

"Hello, Aunt Laurel, it's Leo," he said once his call was put through. Standard practice was to assume the switchboard operators were always listening in, which was why sensitive information was usually delivered in code or by messenger, but they had certain set phrases that got the job done and wouldn't stand out to eavesdroppers.

"I hope you're well," she said unconvincingly, perhaps explaining why she had a desk job rather than a field assignment.

"I hate to call so early, but I'm here on work for the Home Office and forgot to pack that book by my bedside." This meant he needed Templeton to establish his bona fides with all the appropriate bureaucrats.

"Oh. I'll get on that," she said, not bothering to suppress a yawn. "Your uncle's not happy with you."

Leo grit his teeth. "Well, I'm not happy with him, either. You might let him know that—" He broke off. There was only so much he could say on the telephone.

After disconnecting, he lingered a moment at the receptionist's desk, fingering the battered wire paper trays that sat on the scarred wooden surface of the desk. He looked out at the small waiting area with its moss green linoleum floors and its walls that had been distempered a slightly paler shade of green. The room couldn't be mistaken for anything but the surgery of a country doctor, and Leo could see why the very typicality of the place was comforting to James.

Leo tiptoed upstairs, trying not to wake the doctor. He erased all traces of himself from James's bedroom and rumpled the sheets in the spare room. Then he neatly made the bed. He was fairly certain that Leo Page, church window enthusiast or Home Office specialist or whatever he was supposed to be, wouldn't leave an unmade bed.

"What was the point in rumpling the sheets if you were only going to make the bed?" James asked from the doorway. He looked weary, which stood to reason after having only had four hours of sleep, interrupted by bad dreams. Or, at least, they had seemed pretty damned unpleasant to Leo, who had only had to experience them second-hand. Still, James looked rumpled and adorable, wearing trousers and an old jumper, and something in Leo's heart gave a demented little leap at the sight of him.

"There's a difference between a bed that's been slept in and then made and a bed that hasn't been slept in at all. Your cleaner will know that difference." He deliberately fluffed a pillow.

"She doesn't come upstairs."

Ah, yes. Leo remembered now. James wanted his house to be a safe place he could have a life with someone. He hadn't said as much, but it didn't take a mind as sharp as Leo's to figure it out. This house only made sense if there were someone to share it with. There was a superfluity of furniture, for one: an extra chair by the fire, too many hooks by the door, a bed too large for one man. Even the wardrobe had all the hangers pushed to one side, as if waiting for another person's coats and trousers.

Leo's clothes weren't going to find a home in anyone's wardrobe. It wasn't possible. Not with his work, his constantly shifting identity, his inability to be honest about the basic details of his life. But Templeton had married. He had heard that there was a Lady Templeton and several small Templetons living in a house in Hampstead Heath. And surely other agents had settled down to some semblance of a regular, civilian life. But most people, presumably, started out with mothers or fathers or siblings, so maybe they were in the habit of having people they belonged to, a house they belonged in. He had always counted it a blessing that he didn't expect to have that kind of life. His work would be so much harder if there were people he cared about. But the truth was that Leo didn't even know how to begin to build that kind of life in the first place.

Absently, he shut the wardrobe door. But in doing so, he saw a small trunk wedged behind the wardrobe, where the roof slanted down. It was fastened with a padlock. Leo nudged it with his foot. "Looks like the sort of thing that ought to be marked with an X on a treasure map," he said.

"Oh, that," James said, rubbing the back of his neck. "That's, er. That's my arsenal, I suppose."

"Your—I beg your pardon?"

"Cora's, really. Miss Delacourt. She has a couple of rifles and half a dozen handguns. I'm afraid she's always been fond of firearms."

"Yes, she told me the most shocking story the other day."

"Edith was afraid she might be going a bit dotty. She's long past seventy, you know. And when we were all worried about a German invasion, Cora got into the most disturbing habit of cleaning and loading her weapons every day. She taught Wendy how to shoot. Edith was afraid the two of them would shoot anybody they suspected of being a German soldier parachuting in. So Edith packed up it all up, locked it, and as soon as I came home, she asked me to keep it safe."

Leo didn't know what shocked him more—that fluffy old Cora Delacourt had a small arsenal or whether she had attempted to instruct Wendy, who at the time couldn't have been more than twelve, how to shoot. Although, during the war, Leo had seen people older than Miss Delacourt and younger than Miss Smythe fighting for the resistance. For that matter, Leo himself hadn't reached his fifteenth birthday when he started working for Templeton. It was hardly unheard of—

"Dare I ask what you're thinking to make you grimace like that?" James regarded him quizzically. "Better stop before your face freezes that way."

Leo attempted a neutral expression and stepped forward. He brushed a bit of lint off the front of James's jumper, letting his hand linger over the beating heart below. James placed his hand on Leo's, holding it in place. "Good morning," Leo said, feeling stupidly shy as he looked at the other man's open expression.

James's mouth quirked up. "Good morning," he repeated.

"Look, I'm going to spoil things by asking about the murders."

James stiffened, almost imperceptibly, but he didn't step away and didn't take his hand away from Leo's. "Go ahead."

Leo leaned in, resting his forehead against James's shoulder. He breathed in the scent of wool and hard soap. "What were you going to tell me about last night? You said there was something you ought to tell me."

"Two days a week I'm attending physician at a nursing home in Bourton on the Water. Yesterday I saw Edward Norris visiting a patient who is more or less catatonic." Leo listened as James relayed what he had seen and heard in Dempsey's room. "What I don't understand," James concluded, "is why he'd use a false name."

"Norris deserted." Leo spoke the words into the bristly underside of James's jaw. This was the first time he had ever seen the man unshaved. "During the Tunisia Campaign. He spent time in one of our more ghastly military prisons and then was sent to Normandy."

"And then, after all that, dubious war record and all, went to work for a colonel? That doesn't make any sense."

"No, it doesn't. Armstrong wasn't even his commanding officer. There was no connection between the two men before Norris came here, as far as I can tell."

"There's one other thing. Mary Griffiths' Veronal went missing from her handbag."

"Does she remember when?"

"Unfortunately not. And she truly does leave that bag everywhere. Wendy has to fetch it for her at least once a week."

Leo suppressed a groan. He was starting to get a pretty clear picture of at least part of this case. "All right," he said. "Here's what we're going to do. I'm going up to Wych Hall to sit in on the police interviews. They're going to want to ask Marston whether he saw or heard anything, so you might want to give him a heads up." He felt James nod.

"I'll stop by Marston's cottage after I see my morning patients."

"I admire you, you know," Leo said.

"What?" James asked, startled.

"I know this is hard. And you'd be well within your rights to bar the door and refuse to have anything to do with me. Hell, if I were any kind of friend that's what I'd insist you do, but instead here I am asking you to cooperate."

James pulled back far enough to look Leo in the eye. "Will I see you later?"

"You might not want to." Leo swallowed. "Things are about to get a bit dicey."

James took Leo's chin and stopped him from looking away. "I'm not an idiot," he said softly. "I know that. I also know it has nothing to do with you other than that you happen to be here." Before Leo could protest that this wasn't exactly true, James leaned close. "May I?"

Leo didn't think anyone had ever asked his permission to kiss him, and for a moment he savored the novelty of being treated like something worthy of care. "Please," he whispered, and James brushed his lips over Leo's own. It was just a small thing, barely a kiss at all, but it sent shivers along Leo's skin. He wanted more—no surprise there—but there wasn't time and, moreover, he didn't want to go to bed with James under anything like false pretenses.

"My God," Leo said, "when are we going to get a chance to do this properly?"

"I'm not going anywhere."

Leo, for the first time in his life, wished he could say the same.

Chapter 12

After his morning surgery, James went to the vicarage to check on his patients. He had expected to find the house mostly quiet, with its four inhabitants in various stages of illness. But when he let himself into the parlor, he realized he had walked into an impromptu meeting of the Women's Institute, convened on an emergency basis to discuss the murders.

"There's a madman on the loose," said a middle-aged woman James recognized as the grocer's wife.

"Nonsense, Louise," said Edith Pickering. "A loose madman—" she snorted in derision at the idea "—wouldn't only murder people at Wych Hall. One assumes he'd cast a wider net."

"Richard says it's proof positive somebody was after Colonel Armstrong all along. Poor Mrs. Hoggett's death must have been meant for the colonel," said a third woman, who was holding an infant.

"How does a person push a woman down a flight of stairs when he means to murder a grown man?" asked Edith in evident skepticism. "Rubbish."

"What I mean is the drugs," said the third woman. "Perhaps they were meant for the colonel."

"But then why the stairs?" asked the grocer's wife.

"Maybe she wasn't pushed. Maybe she was given the drugs and then fell."

"Or maybe it was the other way around. Maybe the colonel was killed because he knew something about who killed Mildred," Mary Griffiths croaked from the sofa where she huddled pitifully, a shawl haphazardly settled around her shoulders. She had spots of color on her cheeks and was plainly trying her best not to fall asleep despite the chatter of women and the clink of teacups.

Everyone fell silent as they turned that idea over in their minds, giving James an opportunity to get a word in edgewise.

"You all need to leave right this minute, especially you, Mrs. Talbot," he said firmly, indicating the woman holding the infant. "The vicar is ill, and if you have eyes in your head, you'll see that Mrs. Griffiths is ill as well. At this rate, the entire damned village is going to have tonsillitis for Christmas."

"Language, James," admonished Edith Pickering.

"Out," he repeated. "The lot of you. And you," he said to Mary, after all the women but Edith had left, "get in bed. I don't want to see you on your feet for the next forty-eight hours." He checked her throat—bright red with the telltale white patches of streptococcus, damn it—took her temperature, and sent her to rest in the spare room where she and her husband wouldn't disturb—or, god forbid, reinfect—one another.

After the vicar's wife shuffled upstairs, James turned to Edith. "How is Wendy?" he asked. "She seemed poorly yesterday."

"I daresay she's fallen ill as well." She sighed. "She fell asleep as soon as her head hit the pillow, and she woke up so late this morning the chickens were quite beside themselves. Cora's sitting with her now."

"Which means Cora will get sick. And so will you." Damn it. "I'll need to get someone in to nurse the Griffiths."

"Well, if I'm going to get sick anyway, I might as well take care of Mary," Edith said, as if daring James to contradict her.

Resigned, he gave her basic instructions and climbed the stairs to see the vicar. "Griffiths," he said, knocking on the door. There was no answer, so he turned the knob and stepped inside. The vicar was asleep, which was good. Approaching the bed, he touched the vicar's forehead. It was feverish, but not worryingly so.

"Sommers," the vicar croaked.

"Any new symptoms?" James asked.

"Not any worse." He made an effort to sit up in bed and James shoved a pillow behind him. "How are Mary and the children?"

"I heard the children making a racket upstairs, so I daresay they've made a full recovery. Mary's resting. It's you I'm here to see."

The vicar waved away James' concern. "How are you, James? Two deaths, both violent. That can't have been easy for you."

James felt himself flinch from the kindness. "I'll live."

Griffiths frowned. "I suppose that with Armstrong dead there's no question but that there's a murderer about. I didn't think, but—" He shook his head. "The police asked me if I noticed anything unusual at that dinner party. I told them that I didn't."

James felt his heart give an extra thud. "And was that the truth?"

"It was. Everything was precisely as it ought to have been. The colonel was droning on about Dieppe to the extent that I thought Cora Delacourt would fall asleep. The secretary attempted to flirt with my wife, which is to say it was a day ending with Y," Griffiths said with total unconcern. "I sat next to Wendy, who had a lot to say about vegetable marrows or turnips or what have you, which left me at loose ends to watch everyone else. I saw Mrs. Hoggett take dishes from the maid to bring to the kitchen, and it was all business as usual. I even saw her drinking from that flask of hers. Nothing in the least unusual."

James agreed—it all sounded perfectly typical of a gathering in Wychcomb St. Mary. "But then why do you seem troubled," he asked the vicar.

"Because there have been two deaths, and that means I've missed an evil element right on my doorstep. Either my powers of observation are lamentably poor, or this evil element is so ingrained into the fabric of our lives here that it's become invisible to me. And, James, I don't know which is worse."

THE WYCH HALL STAFF gave their statements in a small parlor the police had taken over, the room bright with the sunlight reflecting off the fresh snow outside. Superintendent Copley of the Worcestershire Constabulary was about forty, a smallish man with salt and pepper hair and a mustache. He seemed thorough and competent. Leo hadn't decided yet whether he was relieved or dismayed to find he wasn't dealing with a bumbling rustic policeman.

The gardener claimed to have seen nothing amiss yesterday. Indeed, Leo had seen him in the taproom of the Rising Sun, about three pints in at around the time Armstrong was being murdered. Sally Bright continued her impression of a flustered and terrified girl. "Is there a madman?" she asked, eyes round with fear. Laying it on a bit thick, Leo thought, but neither the superintendent nor his sergeant seemed to notice. She explained that she had gone to bring the colonel his customary brandy and had found him dead.

The housekeeper entered the room with an air of outraged sensibility. "Aren't you the man who was writing about the church windows?" Mrs. Clemens asked, ignoring the superintendent and turning instead to Leo.

"Special assignment from the Home Office," Leo repeated for the tenth time that morning. "I do apologize about our little subterfuge." He gave a smile that he hoped suggested that Mrs. Clemens was a woman of the world and would certainly understand that needs must in a circumstance like this.

"Oh, I see. Quite, quite." She eyed Leo skeptically.

"By what means did visitors usually enter the house?" Copley asked.

"Guests come to the front door," she said slowly, as if to a recalcitrant child. "Were you under the impression that visitors to Wych Hall slid down chimneys or climbed through windows, young man?"

"Are any other doors used, for any reason?" Copley asked patiently.

"Tradespeople and deliveries go to the kitchen door. But anyone might come that way if they had something for the kitchen. Young Miss Smythe tends to come to the kitchen with eggs, but she doesn't always venture upstairs."

"What about the french doors in the library?" the superintendent asked. "I notice that the terrace they lead out to is flush with the gravel drive at one end. It would make a convenient entry. Did anyone ever call on the colonel that way?"

The housekeeper looked appalled. "Certainly not. Nobody uses those doors but the colonel. He considers—considered—them a private entrance."

Leo remembered the unlatched french door and the spots of wetness on the floor between the door and the desk. "Those doors are customarily kept locked, I suppose?" he asked.

"No, the colonel was accustomed to stepping outside fresh air." That would explain the wetness—just traces of new snow clinging to shoes after a few steps outdoors. But the colonel had been dry from head to toe, so the moisture could not have come from his own shoes.

"Do you keep the front door bolted throughout the day?" Copley asked.

"Only at night, at about ten o'clock, unless the colonel is out visiting or has guests."

The body had been found at nine. "So, the front door was unlocked all day. Somebody could have come in, unknown to you, and either shot Colonel Armstrong directly or hidden, with the intention of shooting him later."

Mrs. Clemens sniffed. "I don't know what kind of house you think this is, with people creeping in and lying in wait." But she didn't deny that a person could have entered the house at any time.

"Did your employer have any enemies, Mrs. Clemens?" Copley asked. "Had he any quarrels?"

Mrs. Clemens appeared to struggle for a way to answer that question in a sufficiently genteel manner. "He was a man of strong opinions. He's been quarreling with Miss Pickering over an easement for decades now."

"What about his staff? It seems that housemaids don't last more than a few months at Wych Hall."

"He was a difficult man to please. I've worked at this house for twenty years. My father was one of his tenants and my sister's family still lives in the village. It is possible that someone without the connections to the Hall and to the Armstrong family might not tolerate the colonel's manner." This all sounded to Leo like a diplomatic way of saying that the man was impossible to deal with.

"Did that include Mr. Norris?" Copley asked.

"Mr. Norris keeps himself to himself. I hardly know the man, for all he's worked here the past year."

"Did he and Colonel Armstrong quarrel?"

"I wouldn't call it a quarrel, no, because that takes two. The colonel sometimes raised his voice at Mr. Norris."

"And how did Mr. Norris typically respond."

"Meek as a lamb, he was."

"Did they have any such quarrel recently?"

The housekeeper hesitated only fractionally. "Yesterday."

"Did you happen to hear any of it? Since you say the colonel spoke loudly during these disputes, I daresay you couldn't avoid overhearing them." Leo suppressed a smile at the police officer's attempt to excuse any eavesdropping on the part of the housekeeper.

"Mr. Norris had gotten a telephone call, and told the colonel that he needed to go to London and wouldn't return until late that night. The colonel didn't take kindly to that. It wasn't Norris's day out, you see. He told Norris in no uncertain terms that he was to return that afternoon or there would be consequences."

"Did he threaten Norris with dismissal?"

"No, that wasn't it." Mrs. Clemens frowned, as if remembering. "He said he'd tell his family."

"He threatened to tell Mr. Norris's family that he was being insubordinate?" Copley asked.

"No." She shook her head. "It wasn't that. Colonel Armstrong said 'I'll tell his family.'"

"Do you have any idea whose family? Or what information he threatened to share?" When Mrs. Clemens said that she did not, Copley told her she was free to leave. The housekeeper left the room, muttering something that sounded like "never in my life," and "disgraceful" under her breath.

Edward Norris was the only member of the household who seemed distressed by his employer's death. He arrived at noon with a suitcase in his hand, and when told about the events of the previous night, seemed genuinely shocked. "I beg your pardon," he said to Copley, "but you mean to tell me that Colonel Armstrong was shot point blank in the middle of his forehead. In his own home."

"We didn't say anything about point blank, Mr. Norris," Copley said coolly. "If you could give my sergeant the details of your whereabouts last night, he's ready to take them down." The superintendent gestured with his chin at a chair, but the secretary remained standing.

"I was in London at the Clifford Hotel on Great Russell Street."

"And what was your business in London?" Copley asked.

"How can that possibly be relevant to your inquiries?"

"Answer the man," Leo said with a pointed look at the secretary. "Otherwise we'll all be here for hours."

"I received a telephone call yesterday morning from a woman purporting to be my sister's secretary and requesting that I visit her at the Clifford Hotel for dinner. But when I arrived, she wasn't there, and the concierge knew nothing of my sister."

"Did you telephone your sister to clear up the confusion?" the superintendent asked.

Norris flushed an angry red. "No. My sister and I have not been in touch for many years. I wouldn't know how to reach her. I was pleasantly surprised to learn that she wanted to see me again, but when she didn't show up, I assumed it was a cruel trick."

So Norris had been cast off by his family, presumably because he had deserted during the war. And last night he thought he had been given an olive branch, but instead had been given—well, somebody had taken care to make sure he had an alibi, was very much how it looked.

"What train did you take to London?" Leo asked. He already knew Norris had been at the nursing home in the afternoon.

"The 10:22."

"That's early for a dinner invitation."

"I had business of my own to conduct earlier in the day," Norris said. Leo supposed this meant his visit to the convalescent home where James had seen him.

"The person who telephoned you," Leo said. "Was it a man or a woman?"

"A woman."

"Did she mention your sister by name?"

"Yes, she said she was Lady Borthwick's secretary," Norris said bitterly. "I was quite taken in."

"When we telephone the hotel, will the desk clerk remember seeing you?"

"I should dashed well think so. I sat in the hotel bar for a good three hours, deluding myself into thinking she'd turn up. Wound up missing the last return train and needing to book a room. And those don't come cheap at the Clifford."

"Yesterday morning, when Colonel Armstrong threatened to divulge a secret to somebody's family unless you did his bidding, to what was he referring?" Copley asked.

Norris went pale. "That's not my tale to tell."

"It's a murder inquiry, Norris," Leo said. "There are no secrets."

"Feel free to arrest me. I'm not answering that question."

"You'll please stay at Wych Hall until further notice, Mr. Norris," Copley said with a sigh.

Later, when the police set off to visit the houses in the immediate neighborhood of Wych Hall to see if anyone had noticed anything unusual, Leo said he'd come along.

"Boy, would I like to know what kind of show this is if the Home Office had an undercover man here waiting for a murder," Copley remarked as they walked through the wood to Marston's cottage.

"It's not as exciting as it sounds," Leo said. "Taxes."

"Oh," Copley said, disappointed but not evidently eager to ask further questions. Taxes were nearly as unlikely to garner additional questions as church architecture was. "I'm only too glad to have the help. There's a crime ring operating out of Stoke Prior that's keeping our men busy."

Leo could not tell if the man was serious, and was still considering whether a place with a name like Stoke Prior could sustain a crime ring, however modest, when the gamekeeper's cottage came into view. He cleared his throat. "I'd suggest going easy on this fellow. He had a bad war and I don't know how he'll react to a man in uniform. Maybe let your sergeant fall back a bit?"

Copley perked up a bit at this. "I suppose it's too much to hope that there's a convenient madman on the premises?"

Leo knew the police wouldn't mind pinning this murder on Marston if all else failed. A forest-dwelling recluse with a beard and bad nerves had to be a policeman's daydream when faced with an unsolved crime.

"Nothing like that," Leo said. "Just a bit jumpy. He was a prisoner of war. And if you want him to say anything useful, you'll probably want him at his ease." Copley hesitated, but ultimately agreed to speak to Marston without his sergeant.

When the cottage door opened, it wasn't Marston but rather James who stood on the cottage's threshold. He had changed out of this morning's jumper and wore his customary tweed suit. "Dr. Sommers," Leo said. "This is Superintendent Copley of the Worcestershire Constabulary," he said, addressing the remark to both James and Marston, who had appeared at James's shoulder.

"We met last night." James nodded in turn to both men, his expression warming when he met Leo's eyes.

Leo felt a surge of daft affection wash over him, and for a minute he felt like he was seeing a friend, not destroying a community.

WITH EVERY MINUTE JAMES listened to Marston answer the policeman's questions, he grew more unsettled.

"I heard nothing," Marston repeated calmly. Well, calmly by Marston's standards, which was to say his hands shook a bit and he startled at every sudden movement and tiny sound. "It was entirely quiet. I didn't hear so much as an owl on the wing, let alone footsteps passing my cottage," he told the superintendent.

Every last sound, James repeated to himself. He had spent enough time with Marston to know the man heard everything: every broken twig, every scurrying mouse. It was one of the invisible scars he carried from the war: he reacted to every noise as if it was a mortar shell or the footsteps of his executioner. So, the man was lying to the police. James didn't blame him for that: saying he didn't hear anything was the quickest way to get them to go away, which was obviously what Marston wanted. Christ, it was what James wanted too.

But James had seen the wetness on the library floor near the french doors that led to the terrace, and he knew they hadn't come from the colonel's own shoes. He had patted down the body himself, God help him, and knew the man was too dry to have been out in the snow. It certainly looked like the murderer had come through the french doors, and if that were the case, he or she could very well have arrived or departed via the footpath.

Marston could be lying to get rid of the superintendent, or he could be lying to cover up for someone. James wasn't certain he wanted to know which it was.

"I'm glad we ran into you, Sommers," Superintendent Copley said as he rose to leave the cottage. "One of my men rang your surgery, but there wasn't an answer. I wanted to get your impressions of the state the body was in when you found it. We had the police surgeon take a look at it, naturally, but it's always good to get the opinion of a medical man who was on the spot, so to speak."

Numbly, James told the superintendent everything he knew about the body. Judging by the coldness of the colonel's skin, he had been dead less than an hour by the time James and Leo got there; the relatively small amount of blood indicated that he had died instantly. There was no gunpowder near the entry wound, suggesting he hadn't been shot at very close range. James had said all these things last night, but had a sinking feeling that he'd have to say them many more times before this was all done with. *If* it was ever done with. He had the sense that it would never be done, that there would be an endless succession of bodies.

It didn't help that Leo Page was there, listening to every word James told the policeman. He wished he had met Leo under other circumstances. It would have been lovely to get to know him without this grisly shadow casting its gloom over them both. He supposed he had always known he wanted someone in his life, someone to share a bed with, someone to bring tea to in the morning. That person wasn't Leo Page, couldn't possibly be. But it had been lovely to pretend.

When the policeman and Leo left, the snow had begun to fall once again, and this time it looked like it would keep up. The entire sky was filled with pale gray clouds, each heavy with snow. James shut the door behind him and turned to Marston.

"I think we're handling this well, all things considered," Marston said as he put a kettle on the cottage's ancient stove.

James smiled at this inclusion of himself. "I nearly fainted when I saw the body," he admitted. It felt good to talk about this with someone who had a similar experience.

"And I nearly got sick at the sight of that policeman outside my door. Glad he didn't come in though. I take it that was your friend's doing?"

"Could be." James would have to thank Leo. "You seem cheerful," he remarked as he took the cup of tea Marston handed him.

"About the colonel dying? I can't say he's much of a loss to me or anybody else."

"Marston, did you know Colonel Armstrong before coming here?" Marston had been a patient at the nursing home where James sometimes worked. When he no longer needed that level of medical care, James had suggested Wychcomb St. Mary as a place where he might get a fresh start. He wouldn't have suggested it if he thought Marston had a former acquaintance in the village. But he remembered the way Armstrong had been startled during Mrs. Hoggett's burial. At the time, he assumed the man had seen Leo, or had been startled by the Griffiths children. But he may have been looking toward Marston, who he wouldn't necessarily have seen up close before that day.

Marston regarded him for a long moment. "We crossed paths."

"He was involved in Dieppe, wasn't he?" James sat heavily on the bare oak chair by Marston's hearth. He hadn't put it together until Griffiths mentioned that Armstrong had been talking about Dieppe the night of the dinner party. "That's where you were captured."

"Armstrong was an incompetent officer. Possibly worse than incompetent. There was always speculation that somebody told the Nazis about the Dieppe raid beforehand. That in addition to being acutely mismanaged and a bad idea to boot, somebody high up the chain of command let a secret slip."

"You think he was a traitor? An informant?" James's head was spinning.

"I don't think he's clever enough for that. It might have been more of a 'loose lips sink ships' situation. And I don't have any evidence that it was him. I didn't kill him. I wouldn't have done, even if I thought I could stand adding another corpse to the world. But I can't get too exercised if somebody thought it was their duty to eliminate him."

"Wait. Marston. Are you saying that's what happened?"

Marston smiled grimly, and James realized it was the first time he had seen the man smile at all. "I'm not saying anything."

"Christ. Did he know you? Did he remember you from Dieppe? Or before?"

"I called on him the day after I moved in. And he said 'bad luck about Dieppe.'"

James needed a drink. "You called—we are *talking* about this later, Marston, but right now—" he shook his head, as if trying to get it to work better. "So it wasn't you that he was startled by at the burial, because he had already seen you. And it wasn't Page. He knew everybody else, so what the hell was going on?"

"That I can't help you with." He lit a cigarette.

"Also, you lied to that superintendent. You must have heard something last night. We both know that."

Marston took a drag from his cigarette, regarding James levelly as he did so. "Listen, I'll deny this if the police ask, so don't get any ideas, but I have the idea that Wendy went to Wych Hall last night."

"Wendy?" James was taken aback. "Miss Pickering just told me that she's been sick in bed since yesterday afternoon. What makes you think she went to the hall?"

"You remember how for the first few months I was here, I jumped at every last noise that came from outside. Well, there some noises I've learned to—not tune out, because that'll never happen, but not jump at, at least. And one of those sounds is Wendy's bicycle going along the footpath. Around eight or nine o'clock, I thought to myself, it's awfully late for Wendy to be traipsing about, and I made up my mind to speak to her about it the next day." He took another puff on his cigarette. "She does often prowl around at night, but usually not on her bicycle. Honestly, I can't tell you more. But I wouldn't even if I could."

Chapter 13

When James next saw Leo, the sun had begun to dip low toward the horizon, and there was enough snow on the ground to make him wish he had worn sturdier shoes. They were at the place where the path forked in the woods, leading to the village in one direction and Little Briars in the other.

"I have had no fewer than seven cups of tea today," Leo said. "I have never had so much tea in my life. Nobody has, in fact. Can a man die of tea poisoning?"

"Well, if you're headed to Little Briars, as I am, you're only going to get more tea. So brace yourself." They walked up the path together, their shoulders occasionally bumping together. "Before we get inside, I ought to tell you that Marston wasn't strictly forthcoming with the police. He believes he heard a bicycle go past his cottage last night. He thought it was Wendy because nobody else is in the habit of bicycling along the footpath."

"I don't suppose he recalled the time."

"Around eight or nine. But in any event, it can't have been Wendy's bicycle. Miss Pickering assures me that Wendy has been quite ill and hasn't left her bed. That's why I'm here, in fact. I would have been here sooner if half the village didn't fancy themselves at death's door due to tonsillitis."

James knocked on the door and Edith answered it herself.

"I tried to keep her in bed," Edith said by way of greeting. "But she's not hearing it." She led the way to the parlor, where

Cora sat in her customary chair and Wendy was curled on the sofa, her face gray and dark circles beneath her eyes.

"Good God," James said. "You were quite all right yesterday afternoon." In the graveyard, she had seemed sleepy and perhaps a trifle foxed, but not ill. "Edith said you had been sick, but I had no idea."

"I slept sixteen hours," she said with an air of pride. "And now my head feels stuffed full of cotton wool. I'm as stupid as can be." Her voice was thick with sleep, as if it took great effort for her to form words.

"Which is why you ought to have stayed in bed," James pointed out. He removed a small torch from his bag. "Open up and say 'ah.'" She stuck her tongue out and complied.

When James put the torch back in his bag, she sat up straight. "Do I have any pustules—" she pronounced that revolting word with evident delight "—on my throat?"

"No." James put the back of his hand against Wendy's head. It wasn't the most accurate method of gauging temperature, but at a touch he knew Wendy had no fever. "You don't have tonsillitis." He reached for her wrist to take her pulse.

"Sixteen hours," Leo said. He still stood in the doorway to the parlor. "That's very odd. What is this, some kind of sleeping sickness?"

"Your heart is racing," James said. "Have you had any symptoms other than fatigue?"

"I thought I was going to be sick a couple of times, but didn't actually vomit. My head hurts and I feel very stupid."

"Wendy, are you absolutely certain that you didn't take anything to help you sleep?" James asked.

"I was already half asleep when we walked through the door," she answered. "The last thing I would have needed was a sleeping draught."

"Are you absolutely certain?" James repeated.

"Yes, James. It's not the sort of thing you do by accident. I don't ever need anything to help my sleep. I always sleep like a stone. I daresay it's my clean conscience and all the fresh air I get," she said brightly, followed immediately by a wide yawn. "I wouldn't even know where to find the stuff. Presumably, Edith or Cora have some, but I've never asked for it."

"What are you suggesting, James?" Edith asked.

James tapped his fingers together. "Wendy's symptoms are consistent with a slight overdose of barbiturate. Nausea, confusion, cardiac arrhythmia."

"This is not reassuring," Edith said.

"Have I been poisoned?" Wendy asked, looking somehow both afraid and delighted.

"We need to send for the superintendent," Leo announced. "I saw Wendy drink from Mildred Hoggett's flask yesterday."

James stared. He had seen the same thing with his own eyes: Wendy drinking from the dead woman's flask, first at the funeral, and then the previous day. "The vicar told me he saw Mrs. Hoggett drink from the flask during the dinner party. I ought to have realized as soon as Griffiths told me, but we've had so much else to think about. How on earth did the flask get back here for Wendy to find in Mrs. Hoggett's bedroom before the funeral?"

"That could be how Mrs. Hoggett was given the Veronal," Cora said, speaking for the first time since James and Leo had entered the parlor. "The timing works out. Someone might have laced the gin in the flask with Veronal, then kept an eye on poor Mrs. Hoggett. After she became drowsy, they might have suggested she lie down upstairs."

"Then it would have to be Armstrong or Norris," James said. "And they're both out of it because one is dead and the other has an alibi for last night's murder."

"There's no saying the two deaths were caused by the same hand," Leo said. James felt even more stricken.

Cora cleared her throat. "Anyone at that party might have suggested that Mrs. Hoggett lie down. We all knew her, you see. 'Oh Mildred dear, you must be falling ill, do lie down in the spare room upstairs and I'll let the colonel know you're unwell.' Just like that. They could even have offered to walk her to the spare room, pocketed the flask, then tripped her once they reached the top of the stairs."

"But how did the murderer bring the flask back here?" James asked.

"People come and go from this house all hours of the day," Edith pointed out. "Anyone might go upstairs under the pretext of using the washroom."

James sank into the empty half of the sofa beside Wendy. "Oh, how stupid of me. I only just now realized. If the Veronal was in Mrs. Hoggett's flask, that means she was the target all along. But the colonel was killed anyway. Does that mean this isn't over? Are people going to keep getting killed?" He truly didn't think he could keep going like this, corpses popping up all over his village.

"No it does not," Leo said, coming to stand behind him. "Not if I have anything to say about it."

ALL LEO'S INSTINCTS, born of years spent sniffing out secrets, told him that Little Briars had the answers he needed. He had worked at the edges of this tangle, pitifully eager not to ruin the surrounding fabric, and what he was left with was a knot the exact size and shape of Little Briars. He ought to have puzzled this out days ago, but his judgment had been clouded, his impartiality compromised, and he had had nobody to blame but himself.

But now he saw the solution and a way to resolve it. When James stood to telephone the police, he sat beside Wendy. "I need to speak to you alone," he whispered. "And now."

"Oh would you really?" she exclaimed delightedly. "Edith, Mr. Page is going to walk me outside to feed my horrible, lazy chickens." That, Leo supposed, was as good a cover as any. He helped bundle Wendy into a men's overcoat and a pair of Wellingtons. With Wendy leaning heavily on his arm, they stepped outside. "Well," she said as soon as the door shut behind them. "You've piqued my curiosity."

"And you mine. I gather that you feel at loose ends here in this village and perhaps you don't think you have options, but I would urge you to reconsider doing anything drastic."

She looked up at him in the purest bafflement. "Mr. Page, what on earth do you think I'm going to do?"

He looked at her closely. She did seem groggy and pale, but those symptoms were easily counterfeit. Then again, she might have taken some Veronal after killing Armstrong, relying on the evidence of drugs to provide an alibi.

"The man who came to visit you last month," he said. "The man who claimed to be Miss Delacourt's cousin. Sir Alexander Templeton. I know him. I know he was in the village, I know he came to Little Briars, and I know he's in the habit of recruiting clever, rootless young people for his service. And while it all seems exciting at first—and it is exciting, it really is—eventually you'll find yourself in my position and...I don't think you'd like that. I don't think the ladies inside would like it, or Mrs. Griffiths. I know Dr. Sommers wouldn't like it. There's time for you to reconsider. Whatever happened at Wych Hall last night, we can bury that easily enough. Nobody actually saw your bicycle. But—"

"Mr. Page. Please stop. I haven't the foggiest notion what you're talking about. This man you're speaking of, he came to see Miss Delacourt. Not me. He was some old friend of hers."

Looking at her, Leo would have sworn that she was telling the truth. But no doubt any number of people had thought the same of him. Well, there was nothing for it but to talk to Templeton. Either he had recruited this girl or he hadn't. As far as Leo could piece things together, Sally Bright must have identified Wendy as a prospective agent and told Templeton. Templeton then visited Little Briars to see Wendy himself. What troubled Leo was that Templeton hadn't told him. Perhaps this was meant to be a test for Wendy, to see if she could dispose of a couple of targets without being detected. Or perhaps, Leo wondered, it was a test for himself. From the very beginning, there had been something wrong about this case—too many agents for too small a job, it just wasn't the way Templeton did things—and now Leo thought he knew why.

Wendy had certainly had the means and opportunity to kill Mrs. Hoggett, although he hadn't figured out why Templeton thought the charwoman needed to be eliminated. She could have put Veronal into the woman's flask, lured her upstairs, taken the flask back, and pushed her down the stairs. But why drink from the flask in plain view of everyone? That didn't add up. Perhaps she hadn't killed Mrs. Hoggett, but had only killed Colonel Armstrong. She had motive and means for that as well. She could have ridden her bicycle straight from Little Briars to the terrace at Wych Hall, knock on the french doors, wait for the colonel to answer, step into the library, wait for the colonel to sit at his desk, shoot him, get back on her bicycle, and return to Little Briars. It could be done in less than half an hour. James had said that Wendy knew how to shoot, and if she had been taught by Miss Delacourt, she probably was more than competent. But none of that answered why Armstrong needed to be killed. Templeton had wanted to give the man enough rope to hang himself with; dead, he could provide no evidence as to who was selling industrial secrets.

Unless Templeton had been lying about that as well. Perhaps the business about British steel was only a ruse. Leo's head spun.

"My mistake," he said easily. "Shall we go inside?"

When they returned to the parlor, the police superintendent and his sergeant had arrived to collect the flask.

"I just remembered something when I was standing outside with Mr. Page," Wendy announced to the room at large. "I was feeding the chickens and it all came back to me. I believe I walked in my sleep last night."

Everyone in the room stared at her. "You've never slept walked in your entire life," Miss Pickering said, putting down her knitting.

"No, I'm afraid I do. I've kept it a secret because I'm really quite ashamed, you see. But last night I remember thinking I needed to feed the chickens. So I crept outside and you will never guess what I saw." She gave a dramatic pause. "I saw a man on a bicycle!"

"Are you quite sure it wasn't a dream, Miss Smythe?" Superintendent Copley asked.

"Oh, yes," the girl said with wide eyes. "When I woke up, my feet were wet from the snow."

"I don't suppose you can describe this man on the bicycle," Copley asked.

"He was large. Huge, really. And he had red hair."

"Which you were able to discern in the moonlight," Leo muttered.

"My eyesight is remarkable," Wendy said.

Edith put down her knitting. "You did no such thing. This is the purest taradiddle."

Wendy ignored the older woman. "My sleep is very troubled, alas." She flung a dramatic hand across her forehead.

"Not an hour ago, you told us you always sleep soundly," James pointed out.

"I was ashamed of my poor sleep and afraid it reflected badly on my character."

"Wendy," James groaned. "What are you doing?"

"I have these episodes," she went on. "It's because of my tragic past."

"You don't have a tragic past," Edith remonstrated.

"My tragic past," Wendy repeated firmly. "It makes me forget things. James can tell you that's quite typical of people with tragic pasts."

Leo did not know whether to laugh or cry. He could not recall ever being so simultaneously amused and flummoxed by a case. Was this girl a murderer? A lunatic? A spy? A silly child with a penchant for drama? Or was Leo missing something entirely? He was too close to see this case properly.

He excused himself and grabbed his coat and hat, wrapped his muffler—that blasted muffler, equal parts kind gesture and red herring—tightly around his neck, and stepped out into the still-falling snow. He was going to ruin his shoes and it would serve him right. Without a clear purpose in mind, he headed toward the village. What he ought to do was get on the first London train and talk to Templeton. But it was Friday evening. Templeton wouldn't be at Malvern Shipping and Surety. He'd be at Hampstead Heath with the family Leo was only vaguely convinced existed in the first place. Why hadn't they set up a secure method of communication? With Wychcomb St. Mary being so close to London, it hadn't seemed necessary at first, but now the lapse struck Leo as yet another sign this case had been wrong from the start. No, he needed to figure out what was going on before confronting Templeton. There was no use going to him with loose speculation. *I thought you recognized my muffler, Wendy Smythe is a clever orphan, ergo spycraft.* Templeton would have him thrown into the Thames. Which, come to think of it, wasn't that outlandish a prospect even if Leo's theories were correct.

When he reached the village, he saw that Christmas decorations had started to appear in some windows. In a fit of what could only be maudlin lunacy, he had the urge to put glass balls and paper stars on a tree. He wanted to sing carols he had never learned. His own life seemed impossibly cold and dark and jagged around the edges, and that had been enough before he realized he wanted warmth, softness, light. That was the problem: he had borrowed a bit of light and warmth from James, from the ladies at Little Briars, from the village as a whole. And all he had to give back was cold and bitterness. Because even if he had been wrong about Wendy Smythe, there were only so many solutions this case could have and none of them were pretty.

He was going to ruin the peace of everybody here, James in particular, and that thought wrenched at his heart in a way he hadn't thought possible.

Chapter 14

When he heard a soft tapping at his door some time after the clock had chimed ten, James hadn't any doubts about who it might be.

"The police laboratory confirmed that there was Veronal in the flask," Leo said as he shivered on James's doorstep. It had begun snowing again, with the result that his hat was a ruined disaster and his coat was soaked through. "And the only fingerprints were Wendy's, naturally enough."

"Do you want to talk about this while standing on my doorstep or do you want to come inside?"

Leo smiled wanly and stepped inside. "I wasn't sure if you'd want to see me."

"Then you're not as clever as you look. I'm losing all faith in the intelligence services." James shut the door and reached to help Leo out of his coat, but the other man leaned away.

"You ought to lose faith, if I'm any indication of our brightest lights. Let me tell you how I've spent the last few hours. I accused someone of being a spy, started to wonder if the only person I've ever trusted is trying to set me up for reasons I cannot fathom, considered the feasibility of moving to the Outer Hebrides and raising sheep under an assumed identity—more assumed than usual, that is. Oh, and while accusing that person of being a spy I *told her my agency head's name.*"

"Well," James said, removing the hat from Leo's head and making a futile effort to push it back into shape before hanging it on a peg. "You've been busy."

Leo let out a strangled laugh. "Am I developing some kind of persecution complex? Is this incipient madness?"

James slid the sodden overcoat off Leo's shoulders. "Come into the kitchen so we can dry this out. When you start to suspect people of various bad intentions, are you usually right? I won't pretend to know you inside and out, but you hardly strike me as a man who flings accusations about and drops top secret information without good cause."

"I've been a model agent," Leo said, making it sound equal parts confession and boast.

"Given that," James said, steering Leo to the chair nearest the cooker, "I'm inclined to trust your judgment in these matters."

"No, that's just the problem. This place has ruined my judgment entirely."

"Wychcomb St. Mary?" James asked, kneeling to unlace Leo's shoes.

"Emphatically. Do you know, James, this evening I thought to myself: I would like to put paper stars and glass balls on a tree."

"I see you've reached the heights of depravity." James stuffed old newspapers inside the wet shoes to speed their drying and then tugged off Leo's socks.

"Anyway, I'm here to make an offer. If you want me to back off, I'll do it. No hard feelings. I know I must set off whatever tripwires you've got in your brain, and—"

James took him by the lapels and dragged him down for a kiss. It was a mess of a kiss, lips and teeth smashing together with no order whatsoever, but he thought it got the point across.

"You don't," James said, when he pulled back to sit on his heels. "Set off my tripwires, that is. Murder does, but that isn't you."

"Sometimes it is," Leo said. "Sometimes I'm fairly certain it's all I am."

"That's a fat lot of nonsense."

"Trust me that I'm more menacing when I'm not sad and barefoot in a country kitchen. You don't know how I've spent the last few years."

"I think I can guess," James said. "I mean, really, Leo. I can't demand that everyone I want to spend time with have a clear conscience, especially when we just finished the bloodiest war in the history of man. Nobody's hands are clean." He stroked down Leo's sleeves and took hold of his hands, as if to make the point. "Not mine. By patching people up, I played my role in letting the war go on. I'm complicit. And I think that's partly why I have so many—tripwires, as you call them. I feel ashamed, almost. But at the end of the day, I believe the war was necessary. I believe that killing is sometimes necessary, even though I believe at the same time that it's an abomination. I need to find a way to make sense of that." He took a breath and passed a hand over the stubble on his jaw. "I just know that I want to—kiss you, yes, but also get to know you. So, I decline your offer."

"That's some shoddy reasoning. All you know about me—apart from the tripwire stuff—is that I'm not an insurance clerk."

"Be fair." James stood and eased himself into Leo's lap. Leo sighed into his shoulder, his hands resting easily on James's hips. It was oddly thrilling when someone who could likely incapacitate a man without much effort was as meek and docile as a sleepy kitten. "I also know you aren't writing a pamphlet on church windows."

"Ha. James, I want to be honest with you. I want to be...truthful." He spoke as if he had confessed to craving some unique perversion. James suppressed a smile.

"Tell me something true, then. It doesn't have to be a secret."

"Something true." He paused, as if rummaging around in his brain for something true required an effort. "Well, my name isn't Leo Page."

"I didn't for a minute think it was. It certainly wasn't when I sewed you up in '44."

Leo shook his head. "That isn't what I mean. Leonard Page is the name on my passport—my real passport, I mean. For a given value of real. What I'm saying is that I don't know what name was on my birth certificate or by what name I was christened."

James stared at him for a moment. "How can that be?" How could a man not know his own name? It occurred to him that maybe the reason Page couldn't come up with a truth to share was that he didn't have many.

"I think it might have been Leon Paget. I vaguely remember being called Leon at the orphanage."

"Orphanage?" James repeated.

"Somewhere near Tournai. My mother's sister married an Englishman and took me with her to Bristol when I was six. She said my English name was Leo Page, and she died before I got a chance to ask her if she knew whether I had any other name."

"But people call you Leo Page now."

Leo cocked his head. "People call me by whatever name I'm using on that particular assignment."

"I mean your friends."

Leo stared at him for a long moment, his brow furrowing. "Oh, James," Leo said almost pityingly.

By that, James assumed he meant he hadn't anyone at all. And that, James supposed, was another truth about Leo Page. He didn't stay anywhere long enough to form connections, to learn to care about people or let them care about him in return. It was a miserable way to live, and James thought he could have done better to fall for someone a bit less impossible. But looking at Leo with his rumpled hair and the shadows under his eyes, James knew he never stood a chance. He took the other man's face in his hands and kissed him. "I'll call you anything you like," he said and kissed him again. "Have you had anything but tea today?" he asked a few minutes later, still sitting in Leo's lap. "I have soup." He gestured to the dresser, where two bowls and a tin of soup sat waiting.

"I dimly recall a scone at some point."

James stood, but not before kissing Leo again. "Food first. Everything else later."

"You had already taken two bowls out," Leo said while James stirred the pot. "Who were you expecting?"

"You, you dummy." James couldn't keep from smiling, and when he saw the astonished expression on Leo's face, he had to laugh. "Not expecting, perhaps, but hoping." Leo still appeared stunned, so James changed the topic. "Where does fair Agnes at the Rising Sun think you are?" he asked as he poured the soup into the waiting bowls.

"I sent word that I'd likely be working very late, and that she shouldn't trouble herself with my whereabouts, because Dr. Sommers offered me his spare room again in the event that I needed it. I left my valise by your door."

Reading between the lines, James guessed that Leo had been hedging his bets; he still had the room at the inn in case James didn't want him that night. "You're welcome to stay here, you know. Either in my bed or the spare room," he added hastily. Leo didn't answer, so James wordlessly placed a bowl of soup before him. "Of course, there will be no hard feelings if you want to stay at the inn. I'm only trying—"

"You're a lovely man."

James felt his ears heat and knew he was blushing furiously. He sat across the kitchen table from Leo and entwined his fingers with Leo's. "Your fingers are still cold. You aren't used to winter in England, are you?"

"I've had winters in worse places than this," Leo said, but his voice was too quiet.

James pushed back the damp cuff of Leo's shirt. "You were someplace sunny before you came here. I can see the line where you tanned." He traced his finger along that line, where tawny skin met the paler underside of Leo's wrist, and felt a shudder go through the other man's body.

"It's work that needs to be done. Somebody has to do it," Leo said, as if guessing the turn of James's thoughts.

James wasn't going to argue with that. Instead, he arranged Leo's hands so they cupped the bowl to capture its warmth. "Does it have to be you?"

"It has to be somebody, so it may as well be me."

James steeled himself to ask a question that had been peering around the edges of his consciousness all day. "What does Mary have to do with all this?"

"Mary Griffiths?" Leo seemed genuinely surprised.

"She's hiding something. She and Norris are very friendly, and if it's just a matter of a flirtation or even a full-blown love affair, then, well, I can't say I like it. Griffiths is a good man. But these things do happen. But if it's something else. If it has to do with the murders—"

"Stop," Leo said. "Mary Griffiths seems totally indifferent to the charms of Edward Norris. I doubt she has the energy or the time for an extramarital liaison. I think Norris is lonely, that's all. He spent over a year in prison, and they only took him out so he could be cannon fodder at Normandy."

"That's where his friend Dempsey was injured."

"Was Dempsey originally with the 51st Highland Division in the Tunisia campaign?" Leo asked, eyes narrow.

"Yes, in fact. What does that have to do with anything?"

Leo tapped his fingers on the table. "I'm not certain. It may have nothing to do with the murders."

"There's another reason I'm concerned about Mary. Whoever killed him wasn't a person he was disturbed to see at the french doors. He could have rung for a servant or even called the police, but he didn't. He didn't even raise his voice to give them a piece of his mind about disturbing him."

"Right. Mrs. Clemens would have heard him yelling."

"And there just aren't many people in the village he *wouldn't* have shouted at. Instead, whoever it was, I don't think he even got up to let them in himself. I think he told them to let themselves in. And then the killer stepped inside, shot him from just inside the doorway, and left."

"What makes you say he was shot from the french doors, though?" Leo asked.

James's mouth went dry as he thought of the body. "The bullet hole," he said. "It was very small. Clearly a low calibre weapon. Not, say, a service revolver." James knew all too well the appearance of bullet wounds from that type of weapon. "It looked like it had been fired from some distance, too. Not close range. No exit wound. Minimal blood spatter." He swallowed his disgust. "And if the shooter entered through the french doors and only took a step or two into the room, that would explain the wetness on the floor. Also, the killing had to have happened before Armstrong had a chance to ring for drinks. If the visitor sat down, Armstrong would have rung for tea or brandy—even if his visitor told him not to. He was that kind of man, you understand. All conversations took place with some kind of refreshment."

"So, someone comes to the french door, shoots Armstrong directly in the middle of his forehead, and leaves. A cool customer. Does Mary Griffiths strike you as having that temperament?"

James felt a wash of relief. "No. Definitely not."

Leo finished off the last of his soup and then regarded James. "Something else happened this afternoon. The colonel's solicitor showed the police a copy of Armstong's will. He left the bulk of estate to his sister's children. His sister was Anabelle Owen who had a daughter in 1918 in Australia."

The relief vanished. "I'll tell you right now that I don't know Mary's maiden name."

"But her son is named Owen."

That would explain what Armstrong saw at the funeral that gave him such a turn: perhaps he noticed Owen and Polly's resemblance to his long lost sister. "I assume you have people combing through the records at Somerset house and whatever the equivalent is in Australia. Thank you for telling me."

"I truly don't think she has anything to do with it, but I'll talk to her tomorrow. I would have gone tonight but..." He gestured between the two of them. "My priorities are askew."

"She's quite sick, so I'm glad you didn't. And," he added, blushing, "I'm glad to number among your priorities."

LEO HADN'T COME TO James's house for a warm meal and words of comfort. It was all very disconcerting. He was playing the role of a man people cared about; that was all, surely. But this was one of those times he envied the person he was pretending to be.

"Upstairs," he said when they had finished washing the dishes and setting them to dry on the draining board. This touch of domesticity was too much. He didn't even dare look James in the eye lest the man see everything that was there. Leo was a good liar—no, Leo was the best liar. But all he could think about was the truth, and the truth was that he was much, much too fond of the doctor.

James wiped his hands on the tea towel and brought his fingertips to Leo's chin, tipping it up. Leo had the childish urge to squeeze his eyes shut, as if that would hide him from James's gaze. He didn't want to hear whatever it was that James was about to say. But James didn't say anything. He only leaned in and brushed a too-soft kiss over Leo's lips. "Upstairs," he agreed.

The bedroom was warmer than it had been the previous night. He could hear the radiator going full blast, and wondered if James had done that for him, just as he had put out an extra bowl. Leo wasn't the type of person who could be counted on to arrive for dinner, couldn't be counted on for anything. James surely knew that. Maybe he just liked bad bets.

Taking hold of James's collar, Leo pulled him close, running his lips over the other man's scratchy jaw and the soft underside of his chin. He smelled of carbolic soap and tea, which Leo thought was the most honest thing in the world for a man to smell like, and he was never going to have tea or wash his hands without thinking of this man.

"I want to pretend," Leo said.

James flushed pink. "That's—ah—not usually my cup of tea, but whatever you like—"

Leo pressed his mouth over the other man's to silence him. "I want to pretend that you'll still like me a week from now. After." He heard James's sharply indrawn breath, then felt his nod. "You'll fuck me," he said, trying his best not to let it be a question.

"Is that what you want?" James asked.

"I want—I need—" Leo couldn't find the words to say what he wanted. He could demur by saying something filthy, or by getting to his knees and not giving any answer at all. Instead, he attempted something like the truth. "I want to feel something that isn't..." That wasn't *what?* He didn't know, and James didn't say anything to fill the silence. "I want my body to be used for something good." He had spoken the words before realizing they were the truth. He was used to thinking of his work as preventing harm, preventing people on his own side from being killed. This case had exposed the flaw at the heart of his reasoning: in order for Leo to believe his work was necessary, he had to trust his intelligence. Without that, he was a common criminal. Even without that complication, his job was taking its toll on him. He was starting to see the world as a collection of things he'd never have, of small joys he'd never deserve. Supper with a man who knew him and liked him anyway; hand knit scarves and whispered reassurances.

"I'll see what I can do," James murmured, as if this was a normal conversation. He wrapped his arms around Leo and held him tight, stroking a hand through Leo's hair.

"I don't think I can handle kindness," Leo whispered, and James's hand went still.

"I'm not sure I can be unkind to you," James said.

Leo wanted to laugh, to say *just wait a couple of days and see exactly how unkindly you'll want to treat me.* "I'll take whatever you have to give," he said, and because he couldn't stomach any more conversation, he took James's mouth in the fiercest kiss he could manage. No sweetness, no gentleness. It was as close to a lie as a kiss could get.

James kissed him back, though, and the soft slide of his lips silenced Leo's mind. That was what he needed, just a reprieve from his thoughts. He unfastened the minimum number of buttons necessary to get the shirt off over his head, then kicked off his trousers without any care for where they landed, before turning his attention to getting James undressed. But James swatted away his hands, and instead fell to his knees.

Leo was about to protest, to say he didn't need this, that he was ready to be fucked, to be used, and the sooner the better, but then James's fist closed around him. "Let me take the edge off," James murmured. "You're in a state." Then his mouth closed around Leo's length.

The wet warmth of James's mouth and the teasing touch of his fingers were almost what he needed: a chance to use his body's sensations to drown out his thoughts. But it was too sweet, too kind.

"I told you not to be kind," Leo muttered.

When James drew back, Leo nearly whimpered. "I'm not being kind," James said, the picture of innocence. "This is me being selfish. Taking what I want from you. Using you as I please."

That, somehow, was exactly what Leo needed to give his pleasure the sharp edge he craved. He imagined himself helpless, his own wicked body being used for the pleasure of this good man. Somehow James got him onto the bed and produced a jar of petroleum jelly from someplace. Leo thought of the two dishes on the kitchen table, and the clanking radiators, and now a slick finger exploring the crease of his arse, and he laughed.

"You're not meant to be laughing," James said. He slid the tip of one finger inside him, and Leo gasped.

"You were expecting me," Leo said, panting.

"I told you, I was hoping."

"Very hospitable." Another twist of his finger sent Leo's eyes rolling back in his head. "The charming host," he managed. He felt awash in warmth and sweetness, even as he grew pleasantly helpless under James's hands. "But, ah, don't forget to use me, if that's not too much to—"

James laughed and tugged gently on Leo's balls, causing him to bite back a curse. "How do you want this?"

"You decide."

"Stay on your back, then." He shucked his clothes and knelt between Leo's spread legs.

Leo groaned at the sight of him slicking petroleum jelly over his length. "God, I want you."

"You have me." James pushed the head of his erection inside him, and Leo gasped. Soon, he was babbling, a rush of words that didn't need to be said, his mind empty of everything but overwhelming need and the illusion of contentment.

JAMES RESISTED THE urge to draw Leo close to him, to press kisses to his temples and whisper things better left unsaid. He knew what Leo needed because it was what he needed too—a momentary reprieve from his thoughts, a bit of temporary oblivion. This thing they had together was a terrible idea, and there would be plenty of time later to think about the full ramifications of what they were doing and feeling. For now, he concentrated on the feel of Leo beneath him, the clasp of his legs around James's back, the sounds he made as James thrust in.

He had done this only a handful of times and hadn't ever really understood the thrill of it. Certainly, it felt good, but so did hands and mouths. But Leo had tears in his eyes and an expression of ecstasy on his face. And James was doing that to him. This was what Leo had wanted, and James was giving it to him. He tilted his hips and thrust again, and Leo whimpered.

"I'm close," Leo said.

"Get a hand on yourself," James said. He was trying to make this last as long as possible, to stretch out this holiday from reality. But the tightness of Leo's body and the simple fact of having wanted this so much had brought him to the brink faster than he might have liked. Leo seemed much in the same place, his breathing faster and more ragged than it had been moments ago.

The thought flitted through James's mind that they might have made it even worse, that instead of oblivion they might have cemented whatever bond there was between them.

Leo murmured something unintelligible that sounded like a warning, and James let himself go, the rhythm of his movements unraveling and becoming more urgent. Beneath him, Leo went rigid and the sound that came from his mouth was enough to set James off and bring on the first waves of his release.

He collapsed on top of Leo, their bodies still joined, their hearts pounding madly between them.

"I rather wish it hadn't been *that* good," Leo mumbled, and James laughed softly.

"Next time I'll attempt mediocrity."

"The fact that we both hope for a next time is bad enough, really."

"You too, eh?"

James pulled out gingerly, and wasn't able to resist kissing Leo's forehead.

In the moonlight, James could see the full expanse of Leo's body. Without his corduroy and tweed, he was all sinewy muscle and dark hair. He had dozens of scars, some tiny slashes, some larger gashes, a handful of bullet wounds. Leo had been in earnest when he said that the wound James tended was the best of the lot. Others must have gone without so much as a dab of iodine or a single stitch, judging by how badly they had healed. This was the price he paid for the work he did. In fact, as far as James could tell, Leo did nothing but pay for it. He was alone, maybe even lonely, and if he kept going like this, he'd be dead soon.

Chapter 15

"You don't look so well," James said, silhouetted by the morning light streaming through the window behind him. He placed a cool hand on Leo's forehead, and Leo wanted nothing more than to crawl back into bed with him—but this time just to sleep. "You have a fever. Hold still and I'll get my thermometer."

"You'll do nothing of the sort," Leo said as he stepped away from James's touch and pulled his shirt on. "I'm perfectly fine." He was not fine. When he woke, his throat had the raw feeling he usually associated with chemical burns, but it was the pounding in his head that really distracted him. "It's a cold. And I have work to do, no matter what my temperature is."

James's frown deepened. "Open your mouth. Let me look at your throat."

"It doesn't—"

"Open your mouth," James repeated, and to his surprise, Leo found himself complying. "You've got what half the village seems to have. Half has a streptococcus infection and the other half is murdered. Quite the lovely place. I really ought to insist that you rest."

"Later." When James didn't respond, Leo added, "trust me when I tell you that I've done more and in worse condition."

"Can you possibly think that's reassuring? Now, stop talking and rest your voice as much as you can. Come for supper? I'm making baked macaroni."

"All right," Leo said, knowing it wouldn't happen. The next time he saw James, everything would have come crashing down. James wouldn't care about the state of his throat, and there certainly wouldn't be any baked macaroni.

"Good." James looked mollified.

When James went into the surgery to see to his patients, Leo bundled up in his coat and that blasted muffler. His shoes wouldn't do, though. The snow was several inches thick on the ground and, based on the gray clouds smudging the sky, there would be more of it before the day was through. He found a pair of rather ancient-looking boots tucked neatly beneath the bench in the foyer, and tried them on. They fit. He and James must have worn the same size shoe.

He felt decidedly the worse for wear as he trudged up the lane to the village. His skin was hot with fever and his head was muzzy, but he could get the case wrapped up by the afternoon. Usually, at the end of a case, he felt almost like a machine: he didn't need to sleep or eat, only catch whoever needed to be caught, or more often, shoot whoever needed to be shot. There had been a time when he thought of himself as an arm of justice, but now he knew he was more like a cat bringing home a mouse to leave on his owner's pillow.

This time he wouldn't even have that. There would be nothing to bring Templeton. Leo could see now the resolution Templeton had wanted, and Leo couldn't give it to him. His judgment had been compromised by familiarity with these people, in the same sense that a lifeboat is compromised by a torpedo landing square in the middle of it. It was shot to hell, useless fragments of something that used to have a purpose. Leo didn't know what that meant for him. Would Templeton have him reassigned? Leo didn't even know if he cared. All he wanted was to hole up at a decent hotel someplace warm and nurse his wounds for a bit. Maybe he really would find a flat and fill it with the accoutrements of civilian life. A fate that was too dull to contemplate only two weeks ago, now seemed appealing.

He hadn't gotten far when he realized he needed to sit. The church was right there, so he walked in, hoping he wouldn't encounter a service. But it was empty except for a middle-aged woman polishing the brasses. Leo sank into the rear pew and looked up at the window of the three hares.

Past, present, and future, James had said. All tangled together, cannibalizing one another. This, he felt sure, was a symptom of the fever. He ought to have let James give him some medicine. Endless cycle of hares ran meaninglessly around in their wheel. There wasn't any point to their perpetual loop. Leo sympathized all too much. Maybe that was why he had fastened onto Wendy, thinking that she was in this next generation of agents. He didn't want that for her, didn't want that life for a child too young to decide, nor for James to lose a friend. But it wasn't just present and future; there was the past, too. There were agents who had come before him, people who had given up normal lives to do what they hoped was right and necessary. He stared at the window long enough that his eyes glazed over and the circle appeared to revolve.

And then he knew what he had to do. With a sense of resolve, he dragged his ailing body up the lane to Little Briars. Miss Pickering, upon answering the door, regarded him with unconcealed distaste. "Cora said you'd come."

She had, had she? Leo wasn't as surprised as he might have wished.

"Mr. Page," called Miss Delacourt from her customary chair, where she was swathed in a multitude of shawls despite the heat of the room. "How kind of you to visit. Do have some cake, won't you?"

It wasn't yet ten in the morning. Hardly time for cake. But there was a dish of iced gingerbread next to the teapot on the table by the sofa. He didn't think he could get any food down the raw mess that was his throat. "I'm afraid not," he said. "Are there firearms remaining in the house? I know you gave the bulk of your...arsenal to Dr. Sommers, but—" He realized too late that he shouldn't have implied that he had seen the weapons. It hinted at a degree of intimacy with James that he shouldn't advertise. And yet—these two women would understand if anyone could.

The two women looked at one another, exchanging the sort of glance that Leo supposed conveyed a good deal of information if you had known a person for decades. "I'm not sure that sort of question is necessary," said Miss Pickering.

"No, not necessary," agreed Miss Delacourt.

Leo sighed. "If you only cooperate with me, then this case can be wrapped up and I'll leave you all be."

"Is that what you want, dear?"

Dear? Leo wasn't certain when he had become anyone's dear. "I'm only here to help with the Home Office."

"Yes, we heard. As a consultant." Miss Delacourt tittered and Miss Pickering shot her a look that Leo couldn't interpret. "Is that what Alex is calling it?"

"Alex," Leo repeated, the remaining bits of the puzzle slotting together. "Templeton—" Sir Alexander Templeton had gone to Little Briars. Leo already knew that, but at first had thought Templeton had come for Wendy. "You all but told me," Leo said. "That story about the hat."

"All but!" Miss Pickering exclaimed. "Cora served it up to you on a platter. I was furious with her."

"What was the purpose of his visit? I can't imagine he often makes home visits to retired agents." Until today, he wasn't even sure there existed any retired agents.

"Oh, to make sure I hadn't gone batty with age. He's got his knickers in a twist—"

"Cora!"

"—about MI6. He needed to know if I was a liability. What if there was a barmy old lady in the Cotswolds telling tales of all the seedier missions we went on? It would make him look very bad indeed, knowing he had sent a girl to crawl into bed with diplomats and smother them in their sleep, that sort of thing. Unsavory, you know."

"Cora, you're going to give the poor man a fit," Edith remonstrated. "He's gone as white as a sheet. I'm too old to dig graves in the frozen ground."

"That's just the fever," Leo said, inanely. "I take it you can still ride a bicycle."

"Of course I can," Miss Delacourt said proudly.

"I thought you could hardly walk. You're always in that chair."

"That's because I've grown lazy in my retirement. We spent so long running our legs off. I've earned this chair. When you've done the sort of work that we have—it isn't too presumptuous to say we, is it Mr. Page? —it would have been easy to decide that I didn't deserve a good life. But I had Edith by my side, insisting that I deserved overstuffed chairs and cake around the clock."

"And so you do," said Miss Pickering gruffly. "I still cannot believe you rode that bicycle. It's shocking. What if you had slipped on the ice and fallen? Who would have found you?"

Leo interrupted. "I thought Templeton came here to recruit Wendy. She's exactly the sort of person he goes after—no background, no family, minimal scruples, quick wits."

"But Wendy does have a family," Miss Delacourt said. "Surely you know that."

Leo frowned. "When Wendy was billeted here—well, that isn't quite right, is it? She never really was billeted here, was she?" He watched their faces for any sign of reaction. The amiable smile never dropped from Miss Delacourt's lips, but something flickered across Miss Pickering's face. "When you took her in, shall we say, did you know who she was? Who she really was, I mean?"

"That rather depends on who you think she is, doesn't it, Mr. Page?" This was Miss Delacourt, in her usual pleasant tone. But Leo caught a shrewdness behind the sweet old lady front.

"She's Mrs. Griffiths' sister. I ought to have caught the resemblance straight away, and as soon as I saw young Polly Griffiths, I knew there had to be a connection."

"Their mother was quite unfit," Miss Pickering said. "Mary had been out of the house from when Wendy was small, and hoped the child wouldn't remember her. But she thought Wendy wouldn't want to live at the vicarage, what with the twins being such a handful, and of course, the roof and the plumbing being what they are. So she asked us, and we agreed."

Leo took a sip of the tea that had materialized in his hand. "But what's more interesting is who Mary and Wendy's mother was." Ah, that got their attention. Miss Pickering's teacup rattled in the saucer and Miss Delacourt fixed a very astute gaze on him. "Colonel Armstrong had a sister, Anabelle, who married a Welshman named Owen. Mrs. Griffiths' maiden name is almost certainly Owen."

"I wondered," Miss Delacourt breathed. "I knew there was something."

"The colonel left his estate to be divided among his sister's children," Leo said. "Which means Mary Griffiths and Wendy each get half."

Now both the women were staring at him. "God knows Mary Griffiths could use it."

"It's not Mrs. Griffiths I'm worried about," Leo said. "There have been two murders, and Wendy has benefitted each time. And unless you want her to hang for crimes she didn't commit, we need to come up with a plausible story, damn it."

"I've heard worse, dear. Obviously, you know who killed Armstrong. But have you figured out yet who killed poor Mildred?"

"You mean it wasn't you?"

Miss Delacourt looked scandalized. "I should think not. So sloppy."

"Mr. Page, you cannot imagine what a trial it's been looking after her for the past half century." Miss Pickering had a fond look that belied her words.

"I rather think it was Armstrong himself," Miss Delacourt said. "He's the only one could have tampered with her flask before dinner. He might have taken her aside earlier and said something like 'Oh, Mrs. Hoggett, I've got this top-shelf gin I don't want to waste on this company, so do me a favor and put it aside,' knowing full well that she'd drink from the doctored bottle herself. He might not have counted on her pouring it directly into her flask, but it hardly mattered."

"How did he get the flask back here?" Leo asked.

Miss Delacourt tittered. "That, I'm afraid, was Edith's naughtiness."

"I didn't care for the woman, but I didn't want her to be found dead with a flask by her side. So, while we were waiting for the police to come, I walked over to close her eyes and pocketed the flask. That was before I knew it was murder, of course. I really did think she had drunk herself to death."

"Very naughty," Miss Delacourt reproached. "I suppose you've gathered what Wendy was about with that story she told about sleepwalking."

Leo groaned. "I let it slip that her bicycle had been heard along the footpath. She cares for you very much indeed." He wanted to ask why Miss Delacourt shot Colonel Armstrong, but there were more pressing matters to attend to.

Miss Delacourt nodded. "And we care about her. Now, young man, I think you'd better go find Wendy before she meddles any further."

Leo got to his feet and strode through the house to the back door, where he saw footprints in the snow leading toward Wych Hall.

THE FIRST THING JAMES saw when he left his morning surgery was that Leo had taken his valise. He had hoped the man would return that night. The absence of that bag argued otherwise.

The front door opened, bringing in a gust of cold air and the vicar. "Hullo, Griffiths. You look better."

"I feel better, too. The children are making merry hell at home, but I wanted to stop in and ask you if you've seen Mary."

"No, did she mean to come to see me? I would have called on her if she needed to be checked."

"It's not that. The telephone rang this morning and a few minutes later she came to me and said she had business at the hall and that she was taking the car. At that moment, I was trying to stop Polly from decorating the dog with her paints, so the oddness of it didn't occur to me until now."

"Did she say who her business was with?"

"I rather assumed it had to be Mrs. Clemens, but I just saw the woman walk past the vicarage, so it can't have been her."

James threw on his coat. "Why did you think she wanted to see Mrs. Clemens?"

"I supposed it had something to do with Wendy's scheme."

James began to feel that he wasn't keeping up with this conversation at all. "What do you mean by Wendy's scheme?"

"The bartering scheme. I'm not meant to know about it because clergy are widely assumed to be as innocent as babies, but I think I knew when Mrs. Dinkler's baby got all that fresh milk."

"It would seem," James said with some asperity, "that I am indeed as innocent as a baby because I'm only learning about it now. Please tell me Wendy and Mrs. Clemens aren't running some kind of black market operation."

"Oh, dear me, no. Nothing like that. I doubt it even rises to the level of ration book fraud. As I said, it's bartering. Wendy has seen to it that everyone has chickens and gardens, and she distributes the items as she sees fit. She has a couple of pigs in the ruins of the old chapel at Wych Hall and they're to be shared among the village when they, ah, meet their maker. Mrs. Clemens is only involved because she doesn't let on about the pigs, and because she knows everyone within a five-mile radius."

James looked for his boots, but they were nowhere to be found, so he put on his walking shoes. "I'll go up to the hall right now. I don't care how many pigs and jars of honey and dozens of eggs she means to hand out. The fact is that she belongs in bed."

"Thank you, Sommers."

"While you're here, what was Mary's maiden name?"

"Owen," the vicar said as if it was a matter of no import.

James swore.

"Wendy has her own father's name, of course," the vicar said.

James stilled, midway through wrapping his muffler around his neck. "Pardon?"

"Smythe. Not a nice man, I'm afraid. When he died, well, one hopes the dead meet with mercy as well as justice, but sometimes..." he trailed off.

"This village," James announced, "has too many damned se-crets." And with that, he stepped out into the snow.

Chapter 16

Leo followed the footsteps in the snow, even as the realization dawned that he was going to be very ill indeed. His skin felt like it had been worked over with a rasp, and the state of his head didn't even bear thinking about. He knocked at the door of the gamekeeper's cottage, but there was no answer, nor was there any smoke coming from the chimney, so he carried on down the path. As he approached Wych Hall, he saw that the police car that had been parked on the drive was now absent. This was exactly why people held local police in such low regard, he reflected. He followed the footsteps to the kitchen entrance.

The kitchen was empty and silent. No use cooking for a dead man, he supposed. But Norris, Sally Bright, and Mrs. Clemens were all still staying at the hall. He drew his pistol from his pocket and climbed the stairs toward the library. He wasn't surprised to find Norris sitting on the hearthrug burning a stack of papers.

"Ah," Leo said from the doorway. "I suppose it's too much to hope that you've saved anything I might find of interest."

Norris spun toward the door, a revolver in his hand. "Damn it, Page. Bugger off, why don't you."

"I don't think that's a good idea," Leo said, not moving at all and keeping his posture as casual as he could.

"I'm using this on myself as soon as I finish with these papers. There's nothing to stop me from using it on you first."

"Sounds about right, but may I ask why you're going to top yourself?"

"I'm already a dead man. I'll hang for the charwoman's death, and you know it. And I'm not going back to prison. I can't face it. Maybe that makes me a coward, but so be it."

"Why go to the trouble of burning the evidence if you're only going to kill yourself afterward? When you're dead, it won't matter what people think of you."

Norris gave a bitter laugh. "I've long since stopped caring what people think of me. These papers don't have a damned thing to do with me."

"I see. Your disgraces are a matter of public record. But the papers you're burning don't have to do with you. They're about someone who matters very much to you and who is in no position to protect himself."

Norris cocked the revolver. "I swear to God, Page, if you try to stop me from destroying them, I'll use this on you."

"I don't doubt it for a minute," Page said easily. "Daresay I'd do the same in your shoes. So, Armstrong was blackmailing you. You and your friend spent time in military prison, but it wasn't for desertion, was it? No, don't get exercised, I'd be in much the same situation if I had ever gotten caught. You were put in prison and let out to fight at Normandy. But at some point, the colonel decided he needed an accomplice. He was getting too old to manage a black market steel racket all on his own. He enlisted the help of someone he knew he could control. Threatening to tell your friend's family the true reason he was put in prison, that was the gun he had to your head. That's bad. But I know you didn't murder him."

"That makes two of us, and only two of us. The police don't give a damn about my alibi. The constable who was stationed here is out to lunch. He'll be back in a quarter of an hour. That's when I'll be arrested. And I can't face it. I can't. It's damned hard to kill yourself in prison. I ought to know. So I'm doing it here."

"Fair enough," Leo said. "Before you do that, could you tell me what the charwoman had to do with anything?"

"I didn't kill either of them, for Christ's sake. I have enough trouble without compounding it with murder. I did give Mrs. Hoggett the doctored gin, but I didn't realize what Armstrong meant to do. It was only after the inquest that I understood."

"She figured out what Armstrong was up to?"

"No. I'm not that sloppy. She found Armstrong's father's will, which left the estate to be split between Armstrong and his sister or sister's issue. Well, Mrs. Hoggett knew no such thing had happened, and also knew that Mary Griffiths was the sister's child."

The room was silent except for the fire crackling in the hearth, so silent they could hear the sound of footsteps in the snow outside. Please be Sally, Leo prayed to any gods that might be listening. Not anybody else, above all not the police.

"All right." He said, fishing one-handed in his valise for his passport and flinging it to the floor before Norris. "You're Leonard Page now. Go to America. Dye your hair. Since the war, you've worked at an insurance firm." He pulled out his wallet and tossed it to the floor beside the passport. "References available upon request."

The outside door opened and a voice came from the hall. "Page! Where are you?" It was James. Of course, it was James. Leo's heart pounded in his chest.

"Don't—" Leo started, but James was already in the doorway.

"What in heaven's name is going on here?" James asked, as if the situation needed any explanation. Norris had the barrel of the revolver against his own jaw. The tableau was nothing if not self-explanatory.

"James," Leo said, his voice urgent and low, "go back outside. Get away from here." He didn't want to even imagine how disturbing James would find the impending scene of blood and carnage. To Norris, he said, "Run, damn it. *Run.*"

For a moment, Leo thought Norris would pull the trigger. Then James took a step into the room, waving off Leo's protests. "You have a chance to start fresh—no, that's a lie," James said." There's no such thing as a fresh start, is there? I thought there was when I came here, but there's no putting the past behind you, not really. There's more life waiting for you, though, and you have a chance to live it."

Norris looked about to argue. "Run," Leo said. "For God's sake, man. You can top yourself later if you damned well need to, but I hear tires on the gravel. Take the weapon and run, damn you!"

Norris grabbed the passport and wallet, shoving them into his coat pocket. Then he bolted for the french doors, disappearing across the terrace and the snow-covered garden, headed toward the woods. Leo hoped he was fast.

"Page, what the hell did you just do?" Sally Bright asked, coming up behind him. "I just saw Norris running pell-mell across the lawn."

Leo drew his pistol and aimed it at a spot to the side of the french door. "I must be losing my knack," Leo said, firing the weapon. "I didn't fire in time. A masked man, no doubt a double murderer, got clean away, never to be heard from again. I very much fear he killed Norris. Oh well." He put the weapon back in its holster.

He hadn't played by the rules. But there weren't any rules, there never had been, and Leo knew that all too well. Theirs was a world of fear and chaos, with tiny islands of goodness and hope. A man could go his entire life without encountering one of those islands, as Leo very nearly had until he met James. He wanted to be that, he wanted to be a source of goodness and... mercy, or whatever it was. He could do that for a man who hadn't done anything worse—in a world where values of *worse* could be calculated with any precision—than Leo had himself.

"What the hell, Page. What the actual hell am I supposed to tell the police?" Sally asked, shaking her head and staring out the still-open door. "What the hell am I supposed to tell the boss?"

"You can tell him I quit."

THE HOUSEMAID—WHO APPARENTLY wasn't a housemaid, but a colleague of Page's—stayed behind to give a statement to the police.

"Dr. Sommers has had an ordeal and Mr. Page has an acute case of tonsillitis. Unless you want to be responsible for what happens to them, you'll question them later. I saw with my own eyes what happened in that room, and you don't need any information from them until they've recovered," she told the inspector.

As far as James saw it, the local police had been grossly irresponsible in leaving Wych Hall unguarded, and they could very well continue to be irresponsible by letting him and Leo leave. He put his hand between Leo's shoulder blades and walked him out the door before the policeman could respond. "Come along," he said firmly. "You belong in bed."

"Where are we going?" Leo asked when they got outside. The snow was still falling and both of them had arrived on foot.

"Well, I suppose I ought to find Mary. Griffiths said she took the car, so I suppose she can give us a lift back to the village."

"Mrs. Griffiths is here?"

"We think she came because Wendy telephoned her." He began to walk toward the old chapel.

"Wendy is here too? Of course, she is. Whenever there's mischief, that girl is knee deep."

"You don't know the half of it," James said dourly. They approached one of the ruined walls of the chapel, behind which they found Mary and Wendy, both highly disheveled, kneeling beside an enormous sow and a vast number of piglets. The remainder of the pigs nosed at the contents of a trough on one side of the makeshift pen that had been built from fallen stones.

"Oh, hello James and Mr. Page," Wendy called. "You're just who we need. We'd like to coax this lady into the old tack room, but she's not budging. Piglets die if they get cold, you see."

"And you think Mr. Page and I can lift that pig. I'm flattered, but I'm afraid hauling sows around isn't in my line of expertise. How about you, Mr. Page?"

"I'm afraid not," Leo rasped. James really needed to get him indoors and dose him with elderberry cordial. But he knew better than to reason with Wendy.

"Don't be daft," Mary cut in, her voice equally weak. "We need you to help carry the piglets. The mother will follow."

"Or she might try to trample us," Wendy added.

"The book was unclear," said Mary.

They were both extremely dirty and unkempt, and both wore clothing that could have been stolen from a scarecrow. If James hadn't noticed the family resemblance before, he would have now. "All right, Page, let's grab a pair of piglets each. Today really has been full of surprises." James suspected that at some point the shock was going to hit him, but for now, he felt oddly energetic. They managed to get all eleven piglets into the abandoned tack room, then coax the mother in, while the other pigs looked on in a bewilderment James found all too relatable. Finally, when they were all thoroughly dirty, they made their way to the Griffiths' ancient car, which Mary had parked behind the stable.

"I'm so glad you had the sense not to walk," James said. "You're still quite ill."

"Oh, I used Daniel's old car because I didn't know whether I was going to need to bring home any pigs." Wendy, climbing into the passenger seat, dissolved into uproarious laughter. "What?" Mary asked. "I had visions of bottle feeding a dozen piglets by the fire."

"And you came anyway?" Wendy asked.

"The children would have been delighted, and I daresay Daniel wouldn't have noticed."

James opened one of the back doors for Leo, who shot him a surprised look. "I can walk," Leo said.

"Doubtless there are many things you *can* do, but I will personally beat you unconscious and throw you into the boot of this car if you so much as make an attempt," James said firmly. "I have had a *day*, Leo. Do not try me." Leo got into the car.

"I'm not entirely certain what happened in the library with Norris, but I see that you helped him escape," James said softly once they were both in the back seat, his words drowned out by Wendy's chatter.

"He would have been arrested otherwise. There was enough evidence to convict him, and helping him run seemed a better thing than letting him kill himself."

"So you just...let a murderer go?"

"No, I let the accomplice to a black market steel racket go free. It was Armstrong who killed Mrs. Hoggett. But I ought to tell you, I fully intend to let Armstrong's killer go free. I'm not telling anyone. Not Sally, not my agency head." Leo set his jaw as if he expected James to argue with him. "I'll be out of your hair in a few hours."

"I hope not." James cleared his throat. "I find I don't care who killed Armstrong. I mean, I'm curious, but I don't think it matters in any ethical sense."

"Armstrong was blackmailing Norris for liking men," Wendy called from the front seat. "Did you know that?"

Leo shook his head. "That's not exactly—"

"Mr. Norris likes men?" Mary asked.

"Sweetheart," Wendy said gently. "Surely you noticed his flirtation with you was a bit, well, performative."

"Well, how lowering. I would have flirted back if I had known we were putting on a show. We could have had all the gossips from here to Cheltenham foaming at the mouth."

"In any event," Leo said, "Armstrong doctored the war record of one of Norris's friends, and threatened to tell the friend's family if Norris didn't help him do various criminal acts."

"I really do think that if somebody goes around doing blackmail, they know perfectly well they might get murdered," Mary said. "I can't get too exercised about it. But that only explains the colonel. What does Mrs. Hoggett have to do with it?"

"Oh, she was a blackmailer too," Wendy continued, in tones of one stating the obvious. "She tried to blackmail Armstrong about cutting us out of our grandfather's will."

At this, Mary nearly drove off the road.

"You knew?" Mary stared at Wendy. "You can't have remembered me. You were a baby when I left."

"Please pay attention to the road," James begged. Just what this day needed was a road accident.

"Mother had photographs of you," Wendy said. "You haven't changed that much."

"I ought to have been upfront," Mary said, thankfully turning her attention toward the snow-covered high street, "but I was off my head, and I was convinced that if I did things properly, somebody would come to take you away. I'm so sorry."

"No, no. You were kind." Wendy touched her sister's arm. "And it was good to know that you wanted me here. I didn't realize that you knew about Colonel Armstrong being our uncle. It took me ages to put it all together, based on sly little hints Mrs. Hoggett tried to drop."

The car stopped in front of Little Briars. Wendy leaned over to kiss Mary's forehead. "Promise you'll go to bed now," she said.

"Do you really not mind?" Leo asked James as Mary pulled away and Wendy preceded them up the walk.

"That there's been an explosion in local crime? I mind. I strongly suspect tonight will not see me sleeping soundly."

"No. Well, that too. But I mean do you mind that I'm covering it up?"

"I should damn well think you would cover it up."

"So you've figured it out, then?"

James thought about how Wendy had carried on yesterday about mysterious men on bicycles. He thought of the contents of the locked trunk in his spare room. He remembered that Leo had accused someone of being a spy. "I'm afraid so." But he gave Leo's arm a squeeze, and together they walked toward Little Briars.

Chapter 17

Leo had worked under worse conditions. He knew, logically, that tonsillitis was a minor illness that a man who had persevered despite bullet wounds surely ought to be able to carry on with a bit of a sore throat. But when he walked into the parlor at Little Briars, he was struck with the thought that a man could have a damn fine nap on that hearthrug. Instead, he cleared his throat.

"In a few hours, the police will take my statement," Leo said. "I'm going to tell them that Norris witnessed Armstrong murder Mrs. Hoggett by putting Veronal in her flask, asking her to step upstairs, and then pushing her down. I'll also explain that today Norris and I were held up by a masked man who confessed to murdering Armstrong for possession of confidential documents. This unknown assailant entered Armstrong's library through the french doors, shot him with a small pistol, and left through the same door with Norris as his hostage." He regarded the faces around him.

"Is this when Poirot gathers the witnesses?" Wendy asked. "I'm on tenterhooks."

"No, it's when the witnesses gather to pervert the course of justice," Leo retorted.

"How exciting," Cora said placidly. Edith attacked a ball of mauve yarn with a pair of lethal-looking needles.

"If this is going to take more than five minutes," James said. "I'm going to insist that you sit," and with that, he steered Leo to sit beside Wendy on the sofa.

"So," Leo continued, feeling rather less authoritative on the sofa than he had standing, "that's the story I'm giving the police. The only other person who will be required to corroborate it is Wendy when she gives evidence of the redheaded bicyclist. No doubt that's the same man who held Norris and me today." He took a sip of the tea he found he was now holding. "There is, however, another explanation for the colonel's murder that perhaps the people in this room might like to hear, fanciful though it is. Mr. Marston thought he heard Wendy's bicycle pass his cottage. In fact, Wendy had ridden her bicycle along that path to Wych Hall several nights in a row, so Marston could be forgiven for thinking it was her."

"I was checking on the sow," Wendy said. "I didn't want the piglets to freeze overnight."

"And you've also been bartering," James said.

"I start with eggs or vegetables or some of Mr. Marston's honey, and then trade it for firewood or milk."

"Or ration coupons," Leo murmured.

"Only sometimes! Then I keep trading, so people get what they need. It's not strictly black market," she insisted. "It started when I saw that the children at the vicarage didn't have milk, and Mr. Marston was only eating tinned beans, and one of the tenant farmers hadn't any way to heat his cottage. So I just sort of shuffled around coupons and goods until everyone had what they required. It's not strictly black market," she repeated.

"Good heavens. I wondered how you always had milk and cheese," Edith said.

"And I wondered what you were doing with all those potatoes," James remarked.

"I suggest Marston did indeed hear a bicycle, but Wendy wasn't riding it. In this entirely fictitious scenario, Colonel Armstrong's killer was extremely careful about making sure Norris and Wendy—the most likely suspects—had alibis. They waited until Wendy was accompanied by Miss Pickering and Mr. Norris was away in London. Then they rode a bicycle along the footpath to Wych Hall and straight onto the terrace. There, they opened the french doors, took one step into the room, and shot the colonel."

"From the door?" Wendy asked. "That has to be four yards from his desk."

"From just inside the door. We can tell because the drips of water only went so far into the room."

Edith cleared her throat. "What an interesting story you've been telling us, Mr. Page. Now, I think Cora and Wendy could both use some rest."

"No," Cora said. "I'd like to know why Mr. Page thinks this fictitious person murdered Colonel Armstrong."

"Ah, that's where things get a bit strange. My hypothesis is that Mildred Hoggett found out more than she realized while snooping at Wych Hall. Perhaps she told her findings to someone, not understanding their full import. But the person she told understood that Colonel Armstrong was not only blackmailing his secretary and selling black market steel, but that he was attempting to sell information about British steel production to various interested parties overseas."

"He was always a bad one," Edith said, stabbing her wool with especial vindictiveness, "ever since he was a boy."

"Perhaps," Leo went on, "this person strongly suspected Armstrong had killed Mrs. Hoggett, but also knew there wasn't enough evidence to do anything about it. I suppose that this person, who had killed before when duty and necessity demanded it, thought that she might as well play the hangman one last time. It's an unfortunate truth that people seldom stop at one murder, so perhaps she worried that the colonel's next victim would be someone she cared about."

Behind him, he heard James draw in a sharp breath. To tell the truth, Leo wasn't sure about this last part. He thought it equally likely that Cora Delacourt had killed the colonel because she was going slightly barmy in her old age or because decades of espionage had warped her moral fibers. Leo couldn't decide whether Cora Delacourt was a cautionary tale about what happened when you got too used to killing, or a beacon of hope that Leo himself might aspire to a normal life, surrounded by people he cared about. But he wanted to make the case as generous as possible so life could return to normal for the people in this room.

"I knew it," Wendy said as if none of this was news. "As soon as you started raving at me at the hencoop." At this point Leo was starting to feel that Templeton had quite missed the mark in not recruiting Wendy.

"If only I had the pistol," Leo said, carefully avoiding looking at either of the elderly ladies. "It must be one fine weapon."

"Or perhaps the person who used it simply had excellent aim," Cora answered sweetly.

"YOU," JAMES SAID FIRMLY as they left Little Briars, "are getting dosed with aspirin and put to bed. That can happen at my house or the hospital. It's up to you."

"I wonder where my valise went," Leo rasped.

"I daresay it's in the pig sty. You can borrow my clothes."

"But Dorothea," Leo moaned, and now James was certain he was delirious with fever. "And Rosamund. I *hate* her. And I love her. Country doctors make such very bad choices."

"Are they the piglets? Dorothea and Rosamund?"

"Very rude," Leo said, but he let James lead him home and tuck him in bed, where he remained until the next morning. He slept fitfully. They both did, for that matter, for their separate reasons. But when James reached out an arm, Page was still there, and several times he felt Page reach for him as well.

In the morning, James made the easy decision to cancel surgery. Half the patients would only be looking for gossip, and the other half could wait for the district nurse. Instead, he brought Leo toast and tea and a bottle of aspirin.

"I feel like somebody scoured out the back of my throat," Leo croaked.

"Probably I ought to advise you to rest your voice, but the sad fact is that I really want to talk to you." He set the tray on the bed beside Leo.

"Ah," Leo said, glancing away. James knew he would have an uphill climb to convince Leo of what he was going to say.

"First, when I went out to get the paper, your valise was there with a note from Wendy saying she had found it late last night in the pig pen."

"Does that girl sleep?"

"No, evidently not," James sighed.

"Second, I'd like for you to stay here for a while."

"Until I recover, you mean. Shelter to a weary traveler and so forth, very in keeping with the spirit of the season, I daresay."

James shook his head. "For as long as you like. I don't foresee a point at which I won't want you here, but we've only known one another for a week, and I don't want to assume too much. But also, what I mean is, I don't think you have a place to call your own." He rubbed the back of his neck. "A place where you belong. You could belong here." He saw the look of surprise in the other man's face and quickly added, "If that's something you'd like. Otherwise, forget I said anything."

"I've never had a home, if that's what you're offering."

"It is." James felt like he was holding his breath. "For when you need a home. Even if that's only from time to time. Or if it's always."

Leo stared at him. "Don't you think that might be unwise? Sometimes the truth is ugly enough that you don't want to have to look at any reminders of it."

"I thought I'd feel that way," James said. "I did. But I find that I'm growing fond of you at an, ah, accelerated rate." His face heated, as much from the sentiment as from the knowledge that he was expressing it terribly. "When I look at you, I see the man I'm—well, Page, the fact of the matter is all it would take would be a stiff breeze to push me into outright love with you, and I thought you ought to know that. That, well, that's what I think of when I look at you. Not the world's evils. Which, to be clear, I think of the rest of the time, because..." He tapped his head. "But not in any particular connection to you."

Throughout this miserable speech, Leo pushed himself to a sitting position and regarded James with an expression of dawning amusement.

"Oh, please don't laugh," James said. "I've never done this before. I don't ever want to do it again, either. It's terrible and I'm not good at it."

"I don't want you to do it again, either," Leo said. "I'd kiss you, but I think I ought to keep my mouth well clear of anyone I like for a while. And I do really like you. Same thing about the stiff breeze and all that."

"So stay and let's, er." He gestured between them vaguely. "Let's eat supper and have bad dreams and visit the piglets. Whatever you like. Just don't go."

"We can say I'm renting your spare room," Leo suggested.

"That would do," James said.

"Just promise me, if you start to look at me and think of all the things that wake you up at night, send me packing, all right?"

"Fine," James said instantly. "It's a deal. But consider this. If the old lady who's been giving me tea and biscuits for twenty-five years is a trained assassin, I suppose I might like assassins after all. I might have very positive and warm associations with assassins." He gave Leo a smile that barely moved the edges of his mouth but was enough to make James's heart nearly stop. "I might like them very much indeed."

"I'm not an assassin," Leo said. "Just a regular spy. And not even that anymore, so don't get too excited."

"You really mean to give it up? I know that's what you told Miss Bright."

"Yes," Leo said, sounding almost surprised.

James sat on the edge of the bed. "Do you need to telephone London? Somebody at some ministry or other? To let them know where you are?"

"Miss Bright is managing that end of things. When I feel better, I'll go to London and speak to the man I report to. You know, he sent me here to kill Miss Delacourt."

"What?" James nearly spilled his tea.

"Oh, he didn't say so. He kept telling me to get to the bottom of things by any means necessary. I suppose he was afraid Miss Delacourt had gone rogue and started killing charwomen, and that she'd be arrested and start talking about her time working for him. So, he and I will be having words, but I think that after this debacle he'll be glad to see me go. So will Miss Bright, who will spend days spinning yarns for the Worcestershire Constabulary. Look," Leo said. "I know that the decent thing for me to do would be to disappear into the night, to keep you far away from dangerous people."

"Is that what you're going to do?"

"I never was any good at being decent."

"Good. Thank God. I'd hate to think I was falling for something as dull as a decent man."

Leo smiled and buried his face in the pillow.

Epilogue

On Christmas morning, Leo put on a pair of James's pajamas and read the newspaper while James did a fry up. They ate on the floor in front of the hearth.

"Nobody's questioning our story," Leo said for perhaps the twentieth time in the past few days. "And we haven't heard that Norris was arrested, so I suppose he got away."

They were interrupted by a knock on the door. Leo opened it himself to find Wendy, muffler wrapped around her neck and her bicycle leaning against a snow bank. The streets were clear of snow, but the drifts and mounds didn't show any signs of melting. "I'm on my way to the vicarage," she said. "But I'm under orders to give this to you." She held out a brightly wrapped package.

"Me?" Leo asked stupidly. "Not James?"

"Cora says James can open his in person later when you come for supper," she called over her shoulder on her way back to her bicycle.

If Leo were on a case, he'd assume that this meant Miss Delacourt didn't want him to open it with witnesses present.

Or that it was a bomb.

But no, he didn't think Miss Delacourt would risk James's life. Besides, it didn't feel like a bomb.

"What's that?" James asked, coming up behind him.

"Not a bomb," Leo said. "Probably."

"That's good," James said.

"It's a present from Miss Delacourt."

"Huh. Want to open it?"

Leo knelt before the fire and carefully untied the string, then peeled off the red paper, revealing a wooden box. It appeared to be made of ebony and that was inlaid with lighter wood. He turned it over in his hands, examining it for a catch.

"That's Cora's puzzle box," James said. "Lord, but I spent hours trying to work the thing when I was a kid. I don't think it does open. My uncle said it was a prank played by vicious old cats on unsuspecting clergymen."

"There's something in it," Leo said, rotating the box near his ear. He ran his fingernail over the surfaces, then held it up to his hear again. He slid one of the pieces of lighter wood to the side.

"They all do that, and it still doesn't open," James grumbled.

"You have to do it in order," Leo said, already flipping it over and adjusting panels, sliding some over and pushing some inwards. When he had tried a series and it led nowhere, he pushed the pieces back to their starting position and began anew. He lost track of time while he worked at the thing, but eventually he was holding something that was no longer a cube, but a splayed open configuration of wooden bars. He reached inside and pulled out the tiniest handgun he had ever seen.

"Well," he said, after checking it was unloaded. "She heard me say I'd love to get my hands on the weapon. And it's just as small as I suspected. Must fire pretty damned straight, too. Nothing like this has ever been on the market. I suppose she had it specially made."

"All those years she's had a pistol in that box?" James looked outraged. "I always thought it was lemon drops."

"I suppose she only put it there when Edith announced she was giving the rest of the arsenal to you. Or maybe she put it in the box to amuse me," Leo said, turning the weapon over in his hands. It was the kind of weapon that would only do any good if you aimed perfectly. And that shot in the middle of Armstrong's forehead couldn't have been more perfect if Miss Delacourt had lined it up with a ruler.

But she hadn't sent him the pistol to show off. She didn't need to—they both already knew that she was a frankly terrifying marksman. He tried to imagine why she might have sent it. Partly because he had said he wanted a look at the weapon. But why in the box, then? He put the pistol back in the box and closed the panels so he once again had a perfect, unblemished cube, identical to how it had looked when he had taken off the paper. It was proof that puzzles could be solved without destroying things. He didn't know if that was what the old lady had meant, but that was what Leo saw. Proof that he could go on, somehow, without tearing everything up around him.

"To amuse—well, you do look amused, so hooray for that," James remarked.

Leo got to his feet and placed the box on the chimneypiece, right in the center, in pride of place. It had to stay here—it wouldn't fit in his valise. He still hadn't quite gotten used to the idea that he was able to stay with James permanently, but he liked the idea of a little piece of him staying here, connecting him with the place where he belonged.

"Come here," Leo said, but James was already there, his arms wrapped around Leo, both of them holding one another in the warmth of the hearth fire and within arm's reach of a murder weapon, and it was all as perfect as Leo could have wanted it.

About the Author

Cat Sebastian writes fluffy, steamy historical romances about queer people. When she isn't writing, she's reading. She lives in the U.S. South but also on twitter @catswrites.

Check out her Turner Series for trope-driven Regency-set romances (*The Soldier's Scoundrel, The Lawrence Browne Affair, The Ruin of a Rake,* and *A Little Light Mischief*).

Her Seducing the Sedgwicks series is also set in the Regency period and contains pharmaceutical quantities of hurt/comfort (*It Takes Two to Tumble, A Gentleman Never Keeps Score,* and *Two Rogues Make a Right*).

Books in the Regency Impostors series each features a character with a secret (*Unmasked by the Marquess, A Duke in Disguise,* and *A Delicate Deception*).

Page & Sommers will return in 2020.

Read more at https://catsebastian.com/.

Printed in Great Britain
by Amazon

21932079R00131